D1527059

ALSO BY SAM CAMPBELL

Doll House

ROBBIN' AROUND THE CHRISTMAS TREE

sam campbell

For Mom and Dad

CHAPTER 1

You know those people who can book a flight, shove some toothpaste and extra underwear in a bag, and be in the sky all before the rest of us even have our first cup of coffee in the morning?

That's not me.

This trip had been pondered, poked, and meticulously planned for *weeks* — right down to the best burger joints within a ten-block radius. I'd never experienced the Big Apple at Christmastime, and with an entire (parents-free!) week at my disposal, I intended to pack it full. I figured I'd catch the Saks Fifth Avenue Light Show, walk around Hudson Yards, maybe roam some outdoor holiday markets while sipping the World's Best Cup of Hot Chocolate. You get the idea.

What I *didn't* expect was to be hogtied and nearly abducted while ice skating at Rockefeller Center.

Okay, maybe that's a bit extreme.

Seriously, though, there I was minding my own business, cutting through the crowd of other skaters, enjoying Frank Sinatra's "Have Yourself a Merry Little Christmas" pouring from the speakers...when *BAM!* A tangle of arms wrapped around me and dragged me into a corner of the rink.

Yeah. Definitely not on the itinerary.

As I was listening to Frank and doing my best to bob and weave, I couldn't help but overhear the two teens skating a few feet ahead of me. They looked about sixteen, same age as me, and if they were trying to keep their conversation on the down-low, they were doing a terrible job.

Girl: "We're doing this, okay?"

Boy: "Come onnn. You *know* I'm afraid of heights. Do you really expect me to climb up that massive tree?"

Judging by his accent, the dude was definitely Australian. He gestured to the tree in question — as in, the world-famous Rockefeller Center Christmas Tree tree. The one towering above the entire ice rink. Its thick branches were already wrapped in miles of lights, but even though the sun had vanished hours ago, they wouldn't be lit until the televised ceremony next Wednesday. As we skated past the giant spruce, I craned my neck and tried to guess how insane they both must be.

Girl: "Yeah, I kind of do. That star is too big for one person to steal. You know that."

Wait. Did she just say —?

Suddenly, the girl's eyes flicked back to me, like some sort of jungle cat sensing an intruder. My stomach knotted, and I knew I'd made a mistake. I quickly looked away, anywhere but the backs of their heads, and pretended to play it cool.

Unfortunately, I've never played it cool a day in my life.

"WhoAHhhAAa."

I didn't even have a chance to start fake whistling before four hands grabbed the arms of my blue puffer coat and yanked me forward. We sped toward the side of the rink. Well, they sped. All I did was hold on for dear life while my skates plowed through the ice, like that time I walked the

Biggsleys' Great Dane two summers ago and he pretty much dragged me down the sidewalk. I had scabs on my knees for weeks after.

"What are you —?"

"*Ssh,*" the girl hissed, spinning me around to face the rest of the skaters. She stood next to me — all five feet of her — and kept her gloves clamped around my wrists. She was kind of terrifying, but she also smelled really nice. I kept getting whiffs of vanilla and maybe some kind of flower. "What's your name?" she growled in my ear.

"Nate," I said, hating the small tremor in my voice.

"What did you hear?"

"Huh? Nothing."

The girl saw right through the lie. "What," she said again, "did you *hear?*"

I tried swallowing the tennis ball in my throat. All I wanted was a fun week in the city to eat good food and support my Aunt Celeste's big Broadway debut. It was also an excuse to get away and forget about McKenna, the girl back home in Shady Springs, Virginia, who had quietly broken my heart.

Instead, I was starting the trip off with a bang by getting manhandled by a couple of real-life hoodlums.

CHAPTER 2

The boy seemed nice enough. He was definitely the less evil of the two, if I had to choose. He just stood there with a big black Canon DSLR camera strapped around his neck while the girl continued her interrogation.

"Tell us and we won't hurt the crazy goat lady." She finally let go of my wrists.

We all three directed our attention across the rink, where Aunt Celeste was, sure enough, hunched over behind the clear plexiglass wall feeding Gerdy a Christmas cookie. She was too far away to hear, but from her childish animations, I could tell she was fully engaged in baby talk.

"My aunt?" I started. "I mean — how do you know I'm with her?"

The girl looked unamused, almost bored. "We saw you with her," she said. "It was kind of hard to miss the goat."

She was right. Even in New York City, where there never seems to be a shortage of unique getups and personalities, it was easy to pick out Aunt Celeste in a crowd. Her diaper-wearing pet goat...her mountain of aqua-blue hair...her shaggy orange coat, reminiscent of a yak doused in Cheetos dust... There were many reasons why my mom's baby sister stood out.

In fact, Aunt Celeste had changed her hair color so many times over the years that I couldn't even remember it's natural hue. When I was younger, my cousins and I used to joke that she was Effie Trinket from *The Hunger Games*. Mom would tell us to "shoosh" and insist it wasn't funny, but the tiny smirk hiding in the corner of her lips said otherwise.

"Okay," said the girl. She turned to her friend and started chewing the inside of her cheek, thinking. I could almost see the wheels turning beneath her black beanie. "Here's what's gonna happen."

She sank one hand deep into the pocket of her denim overalls while the other prodded me in the chest.

"Since you seem so interested in our little...*endeavor*...I'm gonna cut you in," she said. I stole a glance at the boy, and he looked just as confused. "Turns out we actually need a third partner, so your nosiness worked out for you today."

"I...I don't think —"

"Meet us back here tomorrow at 10 a.m. sharp," she continued. "Got it?"

The Aussie finally chimed in. "C, what are you doing?" he asked, but the girl held up a hand.

"If he wants to be all up in our business, then he can carry some of the weight. Plus," she went on, "three people means one person stays on the ground as a lookout. No climbing."

"Ah," said the boy. *"Brilliant."*

"Hold up." They both looked at me. "I don't really know what you guys are up to, but I'm pretty sure it's illegal. So, just let me go, and I won't —"

"Where did you say you're from?" The girl had an incredible knack for cutting people off.

"I didn't. But...Virginia," I shrugged.

"Virginia," she repeated slowly, eating up every syllable. "Okay, Farm Boy. I'm gonna break this down for you one last time." She inched closer, filling the air around us with her warm vanilla scent. "You heard right. The plan is to steal that star," she said, nodding toward the tree.

You couldn't actually see the star, though. It was completely hidden beneath some type of white, puffy tarp, like a hollowed-out marshmallow perched on top of the tree's pointed peak.

It was as if the girl had read my thoughts.

"Wondering why she's wearing a stocking hat?" I could only assume the *she* she was referring to was the Christmas tree. "It's the first new star in twenty-one years. The entire city is waiting for its big reveal on Wednesday, but until then, it's under lock and key. Metaphorically speaking. No one can see it. But," she added with growing excitement, "we plan on giving them an even *bigger* surprise."

Nothing more insane had ever entered my ears.

"Like stealing a 500-pound star and ruining Christmas for millions of people?"

"It's actually only 300 pounds." The girl shrugged, almost laughing. "But, yeah. Something like that."

CHAPTER 3

The girl's instructions had been crystal clear.

Step 1: Be at the ice rink by 10 a.m.

Step 2: *Or else.*

I wasn't exactly sure what *or else* meant, but I'd watched enough true crime documentaries to know this whole situation could get real ugly real quick. My family was kind of obsessed. We watched them almost every night after dinner, and like clockwork, every episode was followed by a five-minute speech from Mom.

"And that's why you've got to be so careful," she'd say as she paused the TV. "Especially young people. It's sad, but you just can't trust anyone these days."

Dad and I would nod vaguely, pretending it was the first time we'd ever heard those words of wisdom. But as I sat on Aunt Celeste's couch the next morning, scrolling through my phone while I tried to wake up, Mom's advice suddenly started to hit home. After all, I didn't know anything about those guys at the ice rink.

Were they serious? What if I don't show and they get mad? Will they figure out where Aunt Celeste lives? Maybe they followed us back to the apartment last night. Maybe they have violent tendencies, and if I don't agree to their demands, they'll slaughter the goat.

MAYBE THEY'RE CASING THE PLACE RIGHT NOW—

"Nate?"

I jumped at the sound of Aunt Celeste's shrilly voice. She'd floated into the living room of her tiny one-bedroom Brooklyn apartment, and I hadn't even noticed.

See? Wayyy too much true crime.

"What do you think?" she asked, apparently for the second time, clutching a script for the Broadway musical *Wicked*. "Should I smile *with* or *without* teeth?" She flashed both examples for me to judge, but the only thought I had was that it was way too early for this.

Now, before you get excited and start thinking my Aunt Celeste is some kind of famous, rich actress, let me explain.

She's not.

In fact, she didn't have any lines in the musical. She was cast as one of the citizens of Oz, so she'd be singing and dancing with a group, probably wearing some frilly costume with glitter caked on her face. Which I guess was pretty cool. I mean, at least all those late-night acting classes and community theater roles weren't a *total* waste.

Not that my mom ever saw it that way. When we'd helped Aunt Celeste move to New York City three years ago, she'd spent the entire weekend trying to convince her sister to come back to Shady Springs.

"You could still act at the Playhouse," Mom had said. "But what about a full-time job with benefits? Insurance? We're all getting older, you know...."

I'd been busy lugging boxes up the apartment steps, but it was impossible not to overhear them in the kitchen every time I set down another box of dishes on the linoleum floor. Needless to say, Aunt Celeste stayed in the Big Apple so she could take full advantage of every audition and open casting call the city had to offer — even if it meant teaching yoga and selling the occasional "I ❤☐ NYC" T-shirt in Times Square to make ends meet.

As for the three of us? Mom insisted we drive back to Virginia the very next day, during which time I spent the majority of the ride wishing I could jump out the SUV to escape her nonstop rants of disapproval. That was the first and last time we'd visited.

"You okay, kiddo?"

I guess my less-than-enthusiastic response to her teeth dilemma raised some concern. Aunt Celeste wrapped her silk, tie-dyed kimono around her as she sat on the pile of blankets next to me.

"You look a little…perplexed."

I almost laughed. *Perplexed?* Yeah, that was one way of putting it. Aunt Celeste wasn't exactly the motherly type; her life was devoted to the theater and to Gerdy (who was probably still asleep in her bassinet next to Aunt Celeste's bed), which meant she didn't have a lot of practice when it came to, as she put it, "kiddos."

Mom, on the other hand, could make me feel better without saying a word. Just a comforting smile or warm hug is all it took to pull me out of whatever funk I found myself in, usually when I was battling writer's block or a literary magazine rejected another one of my short stories.

Aunt Celeste? Well…at least she tried.

I glanced at the clock on my phone — 9:07 a.m. If I was going to make it to the rink in time, I needed to get moving.

"I'm fine," I said. "Just a little tired from yesterday, I guess."

It had been a whirlwind. After an eight-hour train ride into the city, Aunt Celeste had picked me up at the station, whisked me back to her apartment to settle in and change into some warmer clothes, and then insisted on trekking back into Manhattan to take me ice skating. Gerdy, of course, had tagged along every step of the way with her fresh diaper and pink leash.

"Actually, I met a couple of people at the rink last night, and they invited me to hang out today."

Invited. Threatened.

I didn't see any reason to get all technical.

"That's wonderful!" said Aunt Celeste. She clapped her hands daintily, like she was at the ballet or something. "But I..." Her hands slowed, until she finally dropped them into her lap. "I can't possibly let you wander the streets of New York alone...can I?"

"Come on, Aunt Celeste. You don't expect me to sit in here all day while you're at rehearsals, do you?" She looked around the living room, as if she was just now noticing the yoga mats and goat toys scattered around the carpet, empty teacups on the coffee table. "I'll be fine," I reassured her. "I'm sixteen. I mean, when *you* were sixteen, Mom said you were growing edibles in the flower box outside your bedroom window and sneaking out at night."

Of course, Mom didn't articulate it quite so nicely when she said it.

Aunt Celeste took the bait. She tapped her nose and then pointed her finger knowingly before sinking back into the couch cushion, giggling to herself.

"You're right," she said. "You're absolutely right. Okay" — She threw her hands up like she'd lost a debate — "okay. You go have fun with your new little friends. Just be safe. And not a word to your parents," she added with a wink.

CHAPTER 4

They were already waiting for me when I arrived, loitering near the top of the steps that led down to the ice rink. The girl had traded her denim overalls from yesterday for khaki. She leaned against a stone wall while the boy angled his camera in every direction, snapping photo after photo.

The girl spotted me first. "Good, you're here," she said, ungluing herself from the wall.

"Welcome back, mate!" The boy couldn't resist taking my picture as I walked toward them. I awkwardly threw a hand up to shield my face.

Even though I'd made the decision to leave Brooklyn and meet up, a few murderous thoughts were still crossing my mind, so I tried to keep the vibes light. "I forgot how weird the subway is," I joked. "Some lady had a snake around her neck. And a guy dressed up as Superman was carrying a bag full of decapitated Barbie dolls."

The boy snorted, but the girl looked like she still hated life.

"Anyway," I continued, "I never got your names last night."

"That's because the goat started upchucking cookies," said the girl.

It was true. After a few bites, the sugar cookie Aunt Celeste had bought at the Rockefeller café seemed to disagree with Gerdy's stomach. She made noises with every lurch, so it was a weird mix of bleating and splashing vomit. Eventually, a security guard came along and shooed them away, which meant I had to return my skates and rush off too.

"That's Gerdy for you," I said. "She loves her Christmas cookies, but they don't always love her."

"Hang on," said the boy, his eyes lighting up. "The goat's name is *Gerdy*?"

"Yeah, my aunt's really into theater, so she named her after some famous Broadway actress. Gertrude Lawrence or something. We call her Gerdy for short."

The girl zipped up her black coat. "Cute. Can we get back to why we're actually here now?"

"The name's Rodney," said the boy, completely ignoring his friend. He shook my hand and offered a smile. "Rodney Donoghue."

His manners seemed to grate on the girl's every last nerve. "I'm Clue," she finally huffed, and I could tell by the clip in her voice that she wasn't planning on offering a last name.

"Clue? Like...the board game?"

"Exactly."

I tried to wipe away my smile as I mulled it over. To be honest, I thought it was pretty cool, like one of those names only movie stars or lead singers in bands are born with. But I knew she'd never believe me if I said that out loud. So I just went with, "Nice to meet you, Clue."

Instead of accepting my handshake, though, she rolled her eyes and began walking away, disappearing into the crowd.

"Wha — where's she going?"

Rodney appeared next to me, still smiling, and threw an arm around my shoulders. "Can't plan and scheme without a bit of caffeine first, can we?"

CHAPTER 5

New York at Christmastime — a tug of war between magic and mayhem. One minute you're chatting with a Salvation Army Santa, dropping change into his red kettle, and the next you're being pushed along by a mob of tourists and stone-faced locals. One minute you're walking past a storefront, where soft carols are spilling out into the street, and then suddenly the air is pierced by honking car horns and cussing strangers. It's a game of give and take. And yet, if you're patient and willing to listen, you can hear the tinkling of silver bells cutting through the noise, almost like a lullaby, reminding us all that it's still the most wonderful time of the year.

"Hello? Earth to Farm Boy?" A tap on my arm broke my concentration. I looked up, a little dazed, and found Clue peering into my face. "You good?"

I closed my notebook and tossed it and the pen into my messenger bag. "Sorry, I was just writing down some things."

For the first time since I met her, Clue looked somewhat interested in what I had to say. "What, is that like your diary or something?"

Rodney jogged back down the sidewalk and stood with us. I guess I had slowed up without even realizing it. Now that I had a small audience, though, it was sort of embarrassing. "It's not a diary," I said a little defensively. "I..."

Why do writers always feel dumb when they explain themselves?

"I'm a writer. Sometimes the inspiration just hits, you know, and I have to get my thoughts down on paper before they disappear."

"You're a writer?" asked Rodney. "That's incredible! What sorts of things do you write?"

I shrugged. "Short stories mostly. Or I used to."

I felt the need to add *used to* because the truth was, my creativity had been on short supply lately. It had been weeks since I'd had an original story idea.

We walked a little further before reaching the end of the block. Giant windows wrapped around a corner coffee shop, and a sign above the green door read JAVA THE HUT. A set of wind chimes jingled as we entered.

"Hey, Arlington," said Clue, nodding to the barista as we approached the front counter. "The usual for me. And just put theirs on my tab."

Arlington was your typical hipster, with round, gold-framed glasses, a manbun, and the world's skinniest mustache. The silhouette of a certain chubby slug alien was printed on his black T-shirt, an obvious nod to the whole Star Wars theme.

"Sup, dudes." He grooved in place to the coffee shop music as he jotted down our orders on paper cups.

After picking up our drinks, we joined Clue at a corner table. "You didn't have to get my coffee," I said, sitting down and dropping my bag onto the floor.

"Don't worry about it." She stayed hunched over some massive scroll she had rolled out onto the table. "I work here parttime, so I get a pretty good discount."

Rodney pulled off his jacket, revealing some type of layered beach-bum combo: a white long sleeve shirt and a tropical button-up. "That's right," he said. "I've drank my weight in Java espressos thanks to this one." He dropped into the chair next to me, and a mop of blonde curls sprang out in all directions as he removed his bright orange beanie.

Yep. Between the hair, the shirt, and the white shell necklace, Rodney definitely wasn't born a New Yorker.

I tested my hot mocha. "So," I said, wiping the foam from my lip, "why exactly are we doing this?"

Because I was still confused. Why was I wasting my trip on some ridiculous prank with a couple of strangers? What was the point?

You know. Besides their not-so-subtle threats.

"To make *history*, mate!" said Rodney.

Clue was even less helpful. All she offered was a halfhearted "what he said," before returning her focus to the paper in front of her.

"Right…"

I fogged up my glasses and then wiped them off with the sleeve of my sweater. Clue was studying some kind of blueprint — and by blueprint, I mean a piece of brown packing paper. The sort of stuff you wrap around shipping packages. Or meat.

Clue had drawn a pretty complex sketch of a Christmas tree in the center, marked up with all kinds of measurements, lines, and yellow sticky notes. It reminded me of one of those evidence boards used in crime shows, where they pin up photographs and newspaper clippings and connect everything with red string to try and catch the perps. Clue pulled a pen from under her beanie, popped off the cap with her teeth, and scribbled a new note in the margins.

"Don't feel bad if none of it makes sense," said Rodney as Clue worked away in silence. "It's sort of her thing."

"What is?"

Rodney gestured to the blueprint spread out before us. "This," he said. "The diagrams. The measurements and equations. Clue loves this stuff. But," he said, enjoying a sip of coffee, "you should see her floor plans and building designs. She could have her own show on HGTV. Isn't that right, C?"

Clue kept scribbling.

"Is all this really necessary?" I asked.

Which seemed to be the perfect question to get Clue's mouth moving again.

Without wasting another second, she capped the pen and calmly folded her hands on the table. "Do *you* wanna step on a faulty branch and drop seventy feet?"

Numerous tree branches throughout the sketch were highlighted in red. Clue explained that they were the "good" branches, the ones strong enough to hold our weight, which she'd confirmed a few days ago when she climbed the Rockefeller Center Christmas Tree by herself. She'd tested the best path and marked each branch along the way with red glow-in-the-dark spray paint.

After giving me the spiel, Clue grinned smugly, clearly pleased with her work, and relaxed into the chair. "You're welcome." She took a few sips of coffee before adding, "Anyway, I'm sure climbing trees is second nature for a Farm Boy like you."

I sighed. "Not everyone from Virginia lives on a farm. Our yard is like half an acre."

"In New York, that much grass *would* be a farm."

"I've been to Virginia," Rodney cut in. "My dad used to sell houses at festivals and craft shows all down the East Coast. I'd ride with him sometimes."

My brain tried to imagine it. "Houses at craft —?"

"He means *bird*houses," said Clue without acknowledging either of us. She had returned to her precious blueprints.

"That…makes a lot more sense," I confessed.

"Uhhh huh."

"Speaking of Dad," said Rodney, "should we head on over?"

Clue finished her last note and then began rolling up the brown paper. "Sure," she said, standing. She slid the paper into her backpack and downed the last of her coffee. "Sorry, Nate. Rodney here" — She gave him a look — "was so excited to get started today that he forgot to bring his share of supplies."

Rodney rolled his eyes as he crammed his beanie back over his curls. "I already told you that Mum wanted us to come back for brunch. Why would I drag backpacks and radios down Fifth Avenue more than once if I don't have to?"

"I forgot about brunch," Clue moaned. She scrunched up her nose like she smelled something awful. "Is your mom gonna try to feed me fish eggs and stinky cheese again?"

"It was caviar and Brie," said Rodney. "And no, after you spit it across the table last time, I think she got the hint."

CHAPTER 6

Rodney Donoghue Jr. was filthy rich.

Well, his parents were. Specifically his mom.

I'd say he and Clue gave me the scoop on Mrs. Donoghue's rise to fame and fortune as we walked those last few blocks to the Upper East Side, but that would be a lie. Rodney actually rapped the entire thing. As in, he spit bars while continuing to snap photos of ornate buildings and the occasional pedestrian. It went something like this:

My mum and dad, they met in university.

Two young strangers, no different could they be.

One from Ohio, one from Down Under.

They tied that knot, but then they had to wonder:

Do we stay? (wiki wiki oh!)

Do we go? (wiki wiki NO!)

Clue didn't even try to stop him. She just shook her head every once in a while and looked away, which made me think this whole rapping shtick was just Rodney being Rodney.

Long story short, Rodney's dad never planned on staying in Australia after his study abroad program. But then he met Rodney's mom at some college on the Gold Coast, and after getting married, they lived there for the next 13 years — until Mrs. Donoghue's mommy blog blew up. Apparently, some New York publishing company discovered her site and wanted her to come run a new parenting magazine.

Six months later, they were flying halfway around the world to start their new life in Manhattan. Rodney was eight.

"This is where you live?"

We stopped in front of a tall stone building — the style of which Clue identified as "traditional art deco" — directly across from Central Park. The Plaza Hotel was still viewable down the street, which meant this was prime real estate. Anyone could see that. And if the Donoghues were living here, then they *must* be loaded.

"Yeah, mate," said Rodney, clapping me on the back. "Come on."

An older gentleman in a dark suit and shiny black dress shoes greeted the three of us at the front door. "Welcome home, Mr. Donoghue," said the doorman with a warm smile. He tipped the brim of his hat to acknowledge Clue and me. "Mr. Donoghue's friends."

The lobby was just as impressive: marble floors, dark mahogany trim, and gold sconces along the walls. As we rode the elevator up, I couldn't help but think about Aunt Celeste's crummy apartment back in Brooklyn. The closest thing she had to a doorman was the one-winged angel statue being choked out by weeds in the overgrown courtyard.

Same city. Two different worlds.

The elevator doors opened with the familiar chime of a doorbell...but Rodney's home was anything but ordinary.

I imagined this is what it felt like to step inside Buckingham Palace — if Buckingham Palace was a penthouse hovering twelve stories above Central Park. The same gleaming marble floors as downstairs continued into the grand foyer; antique artwork in gilded frames (which probably cost more than my mom's new Subaru) lined the cream walls; and directly above us, suspended from the center of the domed ceiling, was the biggest crystal chandelier I'd ever seen.

"You're drooling," Clue muttered next to me.

The click of a woman's heels echoed down a side hall, growing louder as she approached. When she rounded the corner, I knew right away that she had to be Mrs. Donoghue because it was like looking at a forty-something female version of Rodney. Same hazel eyes and same blonde hair, though her curls fell past her shoulders.

"Rodney," she exclaimed, leaning in to kiss his cheek. She gave his arms a good squeeze. "My boy. And Cluenette! Darling, how are you?"

Cluenette?

Mrs. Donoghue's accent was pretty thick —
but not *that* thick. I was sure I'd heard her correctly.
Suddenly it made perfect sense. I'd use a nickname
too if I was saddled with a name like Cluenette.

Clue must've sensed my surprise. And
maybe I was dreaming, but I could've sworn there
was a little pink in her cheeks. "Not a word," she
mumbled through a gritted smile, before stepping
forward and accepting Mrs. Donoghue's hug.

"And who's your friend?"

Rodney opened his mouth to make
introductions, but just then, Mrs. Donoghue's phone
started ringing in the back pocket of her designer
jeans.

"Oh," she said, holding up a finger, "I've
got to take this. Brunch in fifteen, okay?" She
wiggled her fingers. "Nice to meet you..."

"Nate," I said.

"Nate," she whispered with a wink, before
stepping away to take the call.

We followed Rodney up a curved stairway
that wrapped around the circular foyer. My

Converses squeaked against the ivory tiles as he led us to the second floor, bringing us so close to the chandelier that I'm sure I could've jumped off the landing and swung from the crystals.

"Bet you're wondering how much it costs to buy a swanky pad like this, huh?" Clue decided to blurt out once we reached Rodney's room. She grabbed a pillow and flopped down on the foot of the bed. "I know I did."

Of course I was wondering. But I also had these little things called manners, which told me it was super inappropriate to ask, so I just pretended like I didn't hear.

Stepping into Rodney's room was like walking through an art gallery — not just because it was massive, but because every square inch of wall space was covered in photographs. Some illuminated by tiny goosenecked lights attached to the wall above them. Some were as large as posters. Others were no bigger than my hand. All sparkling beneath layers of smudge-free glass.

But what really caught my attention was the far corner of his room, where several strings zigzagged from one navy blue wall to the other. Clothespins were scattered along the strings, and each one held a photo, just dangling there, begging to be viewed and admired. The setup was a far cry from the rest of the framed masterpieces, but I think that's what drew me in. A sort of messy, chaotic beauty.

"My sunset strings."

I hadn't even noticed Rodney admiring the photos next to me.

"These are great," I said.

"Mum is always traveling for work," Rodney explained. "Touring her book, speaking at conferences —"

"Your mom wrote a book?" I couldn't help but ask.

"That's right. It's sort of an extension of her magazine, I suppose. Personal experiences. More parenting advice. Even a few embarrassing stories from my childhood, I'm afraid," he added with a laugh, shaking his head. "Anyway, Dad and I tag along from time to time. I take my camera and try to capture as many sunsets as possible. They're all so unique, see?" He lifted one of the photographs to view whatever was written on the back. "Rio de Janeiro," he read. "Completely different from, let's say, the Netherlands." He pointed. "See?"

It was true. Each image was of a sunset, but none of them were alike. Where one was full of tangerine rays reflecting over the ocean, another was an explosion of pink and dark purple spilling over a snowy mountaintop. Each beautiful in their own special way.

"Dude, you could do this for a living," I said. "Seriously."

"That's the dream." We turned to find Clue stretching on the bed, her hands high above her head as she stifled another yawn. "Isn't it, RD?"

We sat on the carpet while Clue stayed in bed, rolling onto her stomach and propping her chin up with her hands.

"That's the dream," Rodney said. And then, with a sudden surge of energy, he kept going: "I mean, just imagine traveling the world week after week in search of the perfect sunset. Snapping photos. Camping out on the beach. Every day would be a new adventure!"

I smiled because I completely understood. Rodney had a passion, and he wanted to turn that passion into a career. Instead of wasting away in a boring beige office somewhere, he wanted to make the world his office. Part of me was a little jealous. Rodney seemed so outspoken about his goals, and I was the exact opposite. I knew I wanted to be an author. More than anything, I wanted to walk into a bookstore and see my novels on the shelves, to have my words mean something to people. I knew all that. But whenever people asked about my "plans for the future," I always clammed up.

Maybe I could learn a thing or two from Rodney.

"So," said Clue, swiveling her attention to me. She slipped into some sort of baby voice, a childlike whine that reminded me of Aunt Celeste's conversations with Gerdy. "What do *you* wanna be when you grow up?"

CHAPTER 7

Saved by the bell.

Mrs. Donoghue's voice buzzed through some intercom system hidden in the walls, announcing brunch was ready. Unfortunately, I didn't escape the interrogations for much longer.

"So, tell me, Nate," Mrs. Donoghue said as she cut through a fluffy slice of spinach quiche, "what are your plans after school?"

I took another swig of orange juice from the skinny flute glass while my mind raced ahead. Graduation was two years away, but adults never seemed to consider that. They always expected you to have an answer, as if seeing a decade into the future was just the norm. And, I mean, why stop there? Why not go ahead and ask if I've been saving for my kids' college tuitions? Maybe inquire about my retirement plan. Check up on my social security.

I'm just trying to survive high school.

That's what I wanted to say.

"Well," I said, swallowing hard, "if you ask my mom, she'll tell you I should get a business degree so I can help run her catering company someday."

Mrs. Donoghue giggled in her throat, too busy nibbling on her peppered salmon and asparagus stalks now to offer a real laugh.

That was my mom's life, though. She served fried chicken and green beans at weddings, fundraisers, and any other special event that was willing to pay. She made pretty good money too, but it's just... I wasn't passionate about catering. If I was going to spend the next fifty-plus years of my life working, I wanted it to be something I felt in my bones.

Something like writing.

"But that's really not for me," I said. "I've been making up stories since elementary school, and I can't really see myself doing anything else." I shrugged. "I'd like to be published someday. A novelist."

Mrs. Donoghue nodded and took her time chewing, as if she really wanted to think it all over. Or maybe she had found a piece of gristle in the roasted duck.

Finally, she asked, "And how do your parents *feel* about that? I must say, as caretakers, we want nothing more than to set our baby birds up for success."

She patted Rodney's arm, and all he offered was a faint smile; I don't think I'd ever seen him so quiet. Clue, on the other hand, stared straight ahead as she gulped down an entire glass of milk. Probably to keep herself from screaming.

"We want to make sure they'll fly when they leave the nest," said Mrs. Donoghue.

A pretty ironic piece of wisdom, considering it probably came straight out of her *published* book on parenting.

"Our Rodney here," she continued, "wants to take pictures for the rest of his life. Now, don't misunderstand, there's nothing wrong with having a hobby, of course, but your futures will be here before you know it. It's time to buckle down," she said, her bracelets jingling as she placed a palm on the table, "focus, and get a little practical —"

"Natasha, please."

It was the first time Mr. Donoghue had put his fork down long enough to speak. When we'd first come downstairs for brunch, he was already at the table with a tinkering hammer and a half-completed birdhouse spread out in front of him. However, he was quickly told to put the project away and change out of his flannel shirt.

"We don't want splinters in the food, now do we?" Mrs. Donoghue had said.

For some reason, I got the impression that Mr. Donoghue enjoyed annoying his wife.

"Let the kids dream a little," he continued. "Practicality isn't the only way to make a living. Look at you," he said, gesturing to the dining room's floor-to-ceiling windows, which offered an unobstructed view of Central Park. "I don't think any of this came from you doing something *practical*."

Mrs. Donoghue straightened in her chair. "You know as well as I that it took a lot of hard work to get here."

"Of course, sweetheart," said Mr. Donoghue.

He winked at me and then began scooping spoonfuls of sugar into his coffee.

CHAPTER 8

A little while after brunch, I got a text from Aunt Celeste: WILL YOU TAKE GERDY OUT FOR A WALK? IF YOU HAVE TIME. I never understood why she always left her caps lock on. It's like she was constantly yelling or in panic mode or something. Ten seconds later, my phone pinged again. This time it was a selfie of Aunt Celeste and some of her *Wicked* castmates. They were all making duck faces with their lips, which was kind of weird. But very Aunt Celeste.

"Sorry, guys. I've got to go."

We were back in Rodney's room. But just as I was leaving, Clue raced ahead and blocked off the doorway with her arms and legs so that her body formed a human X. "Hold up, Farm Boy," she said. "Where do you think you're going?"

"My aunt needs me to take Gerdy out for some exercise."

Clue rolled her eyes. *"Pampers,"* she said, disgusted. "Of course." She let go of the doorframe and stationed herself right in front of me, until the toes of her black boots were practically on top of my scuffed-up Chuck Taylors.

I hadn't been that close to a girl in a very long time, not since McKenna and I used to hole up in the library together after school and study. We weren't dating or anything, but we were definitely talking. One time Miss Ratliffe, the ancient librarian, popped around the corner unexpectedly, so I quickly opened a book and stood it in front of our coffees, which weren't allowed inside. As we both held our breath, my entire existence focused on nothing else in that moment except the fact that McKenna Scott was squeezing my knee under the table. And she kept on squeezing until Miss Ratliffe walked away.

It was just a nervous reflex, but I still remembered it like it was yesterday. The way her touch sent a surge of warm electricity right into my chest.

Not that this interaction was anything like that. The only thing I could imagine Clue wanting to squeeze was my neck.

"Just make sure you're at the tree by seven tonight, okay? It'll be plenty dark by then —"

"Hang on!" said Rodney. He jumped up from his desk chair and ran into what I assumed was a massive walk-in closet. Clothes, neckties, and underwear started flying as he dug around. Finally, he emerged with a large black backpack and a two-way radio. "Here you go, mate," he said, pressing them into my hands. "The radio is already tuned to channel three, so just make sure you don't change any settings. Otherwise, we can't communicate."

And then he felt the need to start beatboxing, flinging his curly blonde hair around like an insane person, before diving into another rap:

Pff buh tss. Pff pff buh tssss.

Yeah, that would be tragic. *Supa supa* manic.

Turn a knob and you'll put us in a — wiki wiki — full-scale paniiiiic.

My hand froze, holding the radio exactly where he'd left it in my open palm. "You're joking." I looked at Clue and then back at Rodney. "Couldn't we just use our phones?"

Apparently, that was a mistake. Rodney cleared his throat and quietly stepped aside as Clue marched into my personal space bubble again. Without saying a word, she grabbed the radio, stuffed it in the backpack, and then shoved the whole thing in my chest.

"I don't do cellphones."

CHAPTER 9

A chill hung in the air, and the entire forest smelled of wet earth, a fragrant reminder of last night's rain. As I pulled back a curtain of leafy-green branches, water droplets sprinkled off the leaves — and there it was. My first view of The Peaks. A quiet fog still slithered along the base of the blue mountains, but its wispy tendrils wouldn't survive much longer. As the seconds ticked by, a golden sun began to bloom above the mountaintops, scattering light as far as the eye could see. Every shade of pink and orange filled the jungle sky.

I put my pen down, suddenly distracted by the whole cellphone situation.

"It's more fun this way," Rodney had said, just before I took off. "Like we're spies on a secret mission or something."

But I wasn't buying it.

Now that Gerdy had stretched her legs and we were back in Aunt Celeste's apartment, I dug my phone out of my pocket and clicked open Instagram to start searching. Just one problem — I didn't even know Clue's last name. I didn't know much of anything about her, really.

Except for the fact that she smelled nice. And had the personality of a Sour Patch Kid.

I found Rodney's Instagram easily enough. As expected, his entire timeline was full of photography, perfectly edited and deserving of any gallery in the world. I clicked on the people he was following but found no Clues. I even tried Cluenette. (And how many of *those* could there be?)

Snapchat? Nothing.

Twitter? Nope.

TikTok? Zippo.

Facebook? Yeah, right.

It was mind-blowing. This girl had no phone and zero social media presence. I couldn't find one angsty pic of her in a pair of overalls anywhere. If I hadn't seen her with my own eyes, I'd have thought she was nothing more than a ghost darting through the streets of New York.

As planned, we all met by the tree at 7 p.m. in our darkest clothes. The spruce itself wouldn't be lit for a few more days, but there were plenty of lights around Rockefeller Center to drown you in Christmas spirit. Angels along the Channel Gardens provided a dreamy backdrop for dozens of family photos, and The Rink itself, sunken below ground level, glowed such a brilliant white that you almost believed it was still daytime.

Rodney and I hung back in the crowd hovering around the Christmas tree while Clue went ahead. She said she had to "take care of something," which made me a little nervous.

"Sorry about my mum earlier," Rodney blurted out as we waited. "I reckon she'll share her opinions with anybody. You know she's even got one about my name?"

I scribbled in my notebook as quickly as I could. This place was a treasure trove of inspiration, and I didn't want to forget any details. "What's that?"

"She hates it."

I closed the notebook then and looked up. "Oh," I said. "That's…unfortunate."

But Rodney was too cheerful a guy to need sympathy. "Nah, it's all good, mate. She wanted something a bit stuffier, I reckon, like Leopold or Lafayette, but my dad wanted a junior. So" — He raised the arms of his oversized black jacket and shrugged, a dopey grin on his face — "here I am."

"Ouch." I'd known Mrs. Donoghue for approximately eight hours, and my already-not-so-great opinion of her was growing weaker by the minute.

"Yeah," said Rodney, leaning in to whisper, "she thinks Rodney is a name for *bogans*."

But before I even had time to ask what a bogan was, all of Rockefeller Center erupted into mass chaos.

CHAPTER 10

"RUN!"

"WHAT WAS THAT?!"

"EVERYBODY MOVE!"

"GO GO GO!"

The place turned into an actual stampede, like when Scar threw Mufasa into a ravine full of charging wildebeests. (Sorry for the spoiler.) People screamed, and everyone began moving in the same direction — away from a cloud of gray smoke.

I was fully prepared to join the crowd, but Rodney stayed put and seemingly calm. Seconds later, Clue emerged from the rush of bodies, breathless.

"Come on," she panted, a half-grin on her face. "Now's our chance." She turned and headed directly for the tree.

"What did you do?" I asked, as Rodney and I raced to catch up.

"Smoke bomb! I know a guy."

Of course.

Of course this was all Clue. As cops and security raced toward the now-evaporating smoke, tourists and locals alike hightailed it in the opposite direction. One homeless guy whizzed past us with a shopping cart, his yappy dog right on his heels, desperately trying to keep up.

We reached the tree trunk and dived into the shadows of the lowest branches. The strategy had already been set: Rodney would avoid his fear of heights by serving as the lookout. Once we started dismantling the star, Clue and I would pass the first few spikes down to him so he could begin filling his backpack. We'd do the same up top.

Clue cracked her knuckles and rolled her neck. "Well," she said, "time to ruffle Daddy's feathers." Without another word, she reached for the nearest branch and disappeared.

My jaw dropped. "Wait a minute."

I looked at Rodney, and he confirmed with a simple nod. Suddenly, my feet weighed about 10,000 pounds. They broke through the concrete, took root, and held me there.

This, I thought. *This is too much.*

Rodney gave me the push I needed. "Get going, mate."

I blinked, dumbfounded, and somehow processed enough to start climbing. As it turned out, the spraypainted branches proved to be a lifesaver.

"When you say *Daddy*," I called up to Clue, who was a few feet above me, "you don't mean...Emelio, do you?"

"The one and only."

That was it. My brain train nosedived right off a collapsed bridge and exploded into a million fiery pieces.

Emelio Perez — a rockstar in the art and design world. A creative genius. Designer of the Rockefeller Center Christmas Tree's newest star.

And Clue's father.

I'd done my research. The night before, I probably scrolled for two hours trying to learn everything I could about the tree, the star, and what I was getting myself into. Mr. Perez's face was plastered across dozens of articles online; some even showed him standing proudly next to his creation in what appeared to be his studio, though the star was always conveniently hidden beneath a white sheet.

From what I remembered reading, Mr. Perez used to be a mechanic. He ran a small shop in Brooklyn for nearly twenty years, where he tinkered with everything from cars to bikes to antique clocks. "The community's next-door handyman," as one article wrote. He was also an incredible artist. Always had a knack for design, always piecing together bits of leftover materials. Apparently, he got one of his metal sculptures placed in a Manhattan gallery, and an art commissioner was so impressed by his work that he hired him for several pieces.

Mr. Perez quickly moved up in the art world, and eventually — like some sort of weird Cinderella story — he went from obscure mechanic to world-renowned designer.

His star was expected to be viewed and admired by millions on Wednesday. And that's what made me sick to my stomach.

"Clue," I said, "your dad is *the* Emelio Perez. This is his star we're stealing." I imagined the headlines. I imagined us being handcuffed and carted off to prison, Rodney rapping away to keep himself together.

"Thanks for the newsflash, Sherlock," said Clue. "Are all Farm Boys as smart as you?"

I could feel myself clamming up. My sweaty palms struggled to hold on, and the bend in my elbows turned to Jell-O. *Are the branches suffocating me?* It sure felt like it. Every bristly needle dug into my neck, like some weird holdup, and the sharp, evergreen scent quickly began burning the back of my throat.

"Great," I exhaled, forcing myself to keep climbing. "That's…that's just great." I swallowed a wave of nausea. "Who needs college when you can spend the rest of your life eating three square meals a day behind bars?"

"Would you keep it down?" Clue hissed. "And don't get your tighty-whities in a twist. Nobody's going to the slammer."

CHAPTER 11

It felt like we had been climbing for hours. Then again, this year's tree was exactly sixty-nine feet tall — another bit of trivia I picked up from Google. Every muscle in my arms and legs screamed in pain, and the sweat pouring into my eyes burned like ocean water. Every new reach and pull tempted me to give up, to rip off my beanie and call it quits. But I guess adrenaline kept me going.

Plus, there was no way I was letting Clue outclimb me.

The closer we got to the top, the more the tree swayed back and forth, like a skyscraper shifting in the Manhattan breeze. I attempted to look down at one point — big mistake. My stomach rolled into my throat at the sudden reminder of how high we were.

And then the whole atmosphere began to change. We left the shadows of the tree branches and slowly found ourselves in the soft glow of the white dome, like the Pevensie children leaving the wardrobe and stepping into a wintry Narnia for the very first time.

Clue planted herself on the left side of the star, and after wrenching myself up the last few feet, I took the right.

Thousands of crystals covered the star, like the glittering scales of some magical fish. Each jewel cast its reflection across the shadowed ceiling of the dome, and at first glance, you might think you were observing the constellations on a clear night sky—

"Are you seriously writing right now?"

"Whoa," I said, flinching and nearly dropping my notebook into the sea of branches below. "Are you crazy?"

"Me? You're the one drafting *War and Peace* while dangling sky-high in a tree!" She shook her head and began rummaging through her backpack. "I should've known this thing would be welded tight instead of screwed. Good thing I brought this."

She pulled out a small blowtorch — a "cordless cutter" she'd called it while pouring over blueprints — no bigger than a milk frother, one of the leftover relics from her dad's shop. According to Clue, they weren't cheap, but her dad had splurged because he considered it a must for every respectable mechanic.

Seconds later, she stretched a pair of thick ski goggles across her forehead. "Ready?"

NO.

Of course I wasn't. I was never going to be *ready* to commit a felony. I was never going to wake up and think, "Ah, today's the day! I feel like some crime." But what was I going to say now that we were already up there? What choice did I have?

I just nodded.

Clue clicked a button, and a jet of blue flame sputtered from one end of the blowtorch, like a mini lightsaber. "Excellent."

She slid the goggles over her eyes and got to work. The star consisted of twelve giant spikes, each one made of metal and crystal, all radiating from a center sphere. Clue brought the flame toward the first spike, and as it began slicing through the metal, a small shower of sparks rained down between us.

"Stop!" I said, scooting as far back on my branch as possible.

Clue pulled the flame away from the star but kept it running. "What's the matter?"

Looking at her was like looking at a human fly the way those goggles consumed half her face. "Didn't you see all those sparks?" I asked. "We can't do this. We're going to catch the whole thing on fire."

"I know what I'm doing, okay? Just get ready to catch this first spike."

But I couldn't shake the image of a burning Rockefeller Center Christmas Tree — with us trapped inside — from my mind. "Clue," I said, "I don't think this is —"

"Just do it," she snapped.

The blowtorch was so tiny that she had to cut around the base of the spike several times before the metal finally gave way. Once it was loose, I grabbed the spike (all fifteen pounds of it) and dropped it in the canvas bag Clue had set up the first time she'd climbed the tree. The bag was attached to a makeshift pulley system — and by pulley system, I mean a rope flung over some random branch. I raised one side of the rope, fist over fist, and watched as the other side lowered the bag down to Rodney. When he was done loading the spike into his backpack, he sent the canvas bag back up.

We repeated the process all over again. More torching. More sparking. More loading.

Just as Clue was about to start on the third spike, though, I remembered something I'd been meaning to ask.

"Do you know what a bogan is?"

Clue turned off the blowtorch for once and began chuckling to herself. "You been talking with Rodney?" She lifted her goggles, letting them rest atop her beanie, and wiped the sheen of sweat from her face. "Yeah…," she said slowly, like she was easing herself into it. Or maybe she was deciding whether or not I deserved to know. "Basically, his mom never wanted him to be called Rodney. But his dad insisted." She hesitated again, and judging by the way her jaw twisted, it was obvious the next words forming in her mouth didn't taste well.

"She thinks it's a name for white trash," Clue finally said. She shrugged. "That's a bogan."

I know I should've been more surprised, but honestly, I wasn't. Rodney's mom was a pistol. At least, that's how *my* mom would describe her.

"Wow," I said. "She really struggles in the confidence-boosting department, doesn't she?"

Just then, a roar of static filled the air.

KKKKRRRR.

Clue and I both jumped. It was as if someone had turned on a TV with no signal, revealing nothing but a grainy snowstorm. *KK-KKKKrrrr.*

And then Rodney's voice broke through the noise:

"Mates," he whispered urgently. "The Yule logs are burning. I repeat, *the Yule logs are burning*!"

CHAPTER 12

It was the radio.

Rodney was calling us with one of his dad's commercial-grade radios. I still couldn't believe we were using those things, but since Clue apparently had an aversion to the twenty-first century, I guess it was good that Rodney's dad was such a big camper and had plenty of them lying around.

I dug the radio from out of my jeans pocket and clicked the button to respond.

"What are you talking about?"

"Neither of you remembers the code word I came up with, do you?" came Rodney's voice through the static. He sounded even antsier. "I *said* the Yule logs are — oh, never mind. We've got ourselves an emergency!"

Clue yanked the radio from my hand. "Spit it out already! What's going on down there?"

"I'm not sure what they're up to, but two maintenance workers are headed your way. You two need to get out of there right now."

"Are you kidding me?" said Clue. But even as she groaned, she began putting her goggles and blowtorch away.

If workers were climbing the scaffolding, we needed to get going. A baby owl was discovered trapped in the tree a few years before, and it was considered cute by pretty much the entire country. Mom had followed the story online for days.

But something told me finding two teenage thieves wouldn't be as well-received.

"Stop stop stop."

We were about halfway down the tree, and I could just make out the general features of Clue's face in the darkness. She held a finger to her lips. We both froze — her a few feet above me — and listened. Car horns blared down below, and the occasional breeze rustled through the branches.

But that's not all.

A faint clinking noise caught my ear, growing louder and louder with every passing second. Boots stomped against metal. Keys jingled against keys.

The maintenance workers.

Some leftover scaffolding from when the tree was first erected was still standing. Metal stairs connected each platform, creating a silver zigzag from the ground up along one side of the tree. Clue and I held our breath as the workers climbed higher and their voices drifted closer.

"I'll tell you what," one of them said, chuckling. "Christy made meatloaf for dinner last night, and I wouldn't feed that stuff to the dogs."

Both men started laughing, and I could only imagine how badly Clue wanted to chuck a rock at their chubby faces. We got a quick glimpse of them through the branches, only a few feet away, before they moved on.

"What if they're going to check on the star?" I whispered.

It was possible. The crew had left a small metal platform at the top of the scaffolding, just enough space to work in case the star needed any last-minute tweaks before Wednesday's big reveal.

I knew Clue was thinking the same because she didn't shoosh me or kick me in the face. She just kept looking up, watching the workers' every move until their lime green vests disappeared.

Seconds ticked by. Each one more agonizing than the last.

Tick...tock...tick...tock...

We waited for the workers to return, to start their descent, but they never did. They'd taken their insults all the way to the top, and once they looked under the dome and saw the two missing spikes, we'd be done for.

I located the next spraypainted branch below me and got my foot into position. "Should we keep going?"

But Clue held out a hand, her eyes still locked on the branches above. So we waited. And waited. And waited.

"Barry! Look at this."

No.

No no no.

This was it. One of them had looked, and the cops were about to be called. By the time we made it to the bottom, a group of squad cars would be surrounding the tree, and the NYPD would have their handcuffs ready.

"What is it?" asked the one named Barry.

Come on, Clue, I thought. *I know you've got an idea. COME ON.*

But no idea came. No masterplan to get us out of this mess.

"There's our problem right there," the other worker said. I braced for what would come next. "You see this string of lights? They're not even connected. Good thing we checked."

Lights.

Good.

Lights were good.

The pounding in my chest and temples subsided. I closed my eyes, rewarding myself with a few well-deserved deep breaths.

Barry grunted, the lights were apparently fixed, and that was that. The two of them were gone in no time.

CHAPTER 13

I'd never been so happy to have both feet on the ground.

We had planned on getting more than two spikes, but with maintenance snooping around, we figured we'd better quit while we were ahead. Plus, it was nearly 9:30, and Clue needed to be home by 10.

"Miss Mable's staying at the apartment with Mom," I overheard her telling Rodney. "But she'll be leaving soon."

We passed a pyramid of oversized red Christmas ornaments, so, naturally, Rodney whipped out his DSLR and snapped a couple of photos. I did the same with my phone before we trekked further down Sixth Avenue, the two spikes in Rodney's backpack jingling all the way.

"Don't mind me, mates," he said dryly. "I quite enjoy lugging thirty pounds of metal and glass all alone."

I offered to carry one of the spikes, but Rodney swore he was only joking. Clue kept walking, unfazed.

After hearing Clue mention her mom, it hit me: I'd learned so much about Rodney's family (probably *too* much), but Clue's was still one big mystery. Her mom, her background, this Miss Mable person — they didn't seem real. I guess part of me had started to assume the streets raised Clue. That she'd sprouted from the concrete one day and had been making her own way ever since.

But that wasn't true, of course. She had some kind of story, and the more time I spent with her, the more I hoped I got to hear it.

We eventually found ourselves back at Java the Hut — only this time we didn't parade through the front door. Clue led us down the alley *behind* the coffee shop.

"Mind the rats," she said as we skirted around puddles in the pavement.

Judging from the rustling noises that came from inside the various piles of trash stacked along the walls, I assumed she wasn't joking.

There were no lights in the alleyway, but the glow of the city illuminated just enough to keep us from falling on our faces. We stopped in front of a giant metal dumpster, the initials JTH almost completely faded, and Clue tossed the lid back like a pro.

"This is where we're hiding them?" I asked.

Clue wiped her hands off on the thighs of her dark overalls. "Yep. I work here, remember? Mondays, Tuesdays, and Thursdays before school. I know the trash pickup schedule like the back of my hand." She whipped out a black garbage bag from her own backpack. Rodney handed her one spike at a time, and she stuffed them inside. "The dump trucks only come through here the fifteenth and thirtieth of each month. Believe me, nothing stinks worse than milk cartons that've been sitting out for weeks."

I had my doubts, but according to Clue, it was the perfect spot to hide the spikes. She'd "find" them one day during her morning shift and be hailed as New York's Christmas hero — or something like that. Honestly, I still wasn't sure what the point was. But I figured they'd clue me in eventually, when the time was right.

Or maybe I never wanted to know.

Ignorance is bliss, right?

Either way, the plan seemed simple enough, so I just stood there and waited while Clue dumped the evidence, keeping my eyes peeled for any oversized rodents.

CHAPTER 14

Apparently Aunt Celeste hadn't forsaken *all* of her southern roots, because she still went to church every Sunday. (Though her ginormous peacock-feathered hat gave off more "royal wedding vibes" than "backyard Baptist barbeque.")

Finally, I thought. *Something she and Mom see eye to eye on.*

After gating Gerdy off in the kitchen and making sure she had her celery water, a fresh diaper, and all the toys she could possibly want while we were gone, we hurried down to the car so we wouldn't be late for the 10 o'clock service.

"Why don't you just take the subway?" I asked as Aunt Celeste's ancient hatchback — which resembled a tan-colored hearse — puttered over the Brooklyn Bridge. The pleather interior was peeling in rubbery sheets, and the whole thing seemed to be on its last leg.

"The Lord deserves my best," she said, adjusting her rearview mirror so she could check her cherry-red lipstick. "And public transportation is not it."

I'm sure the music was great, and I'm sure the pastor had a lot of applicable points — points that someone like me, a delinquent in training, could really benefit from. But I've got to be honest. My mind was focused on everything *but* the service. I was too busy people-watching. Nearly everyone in the auditorium turned around at least twice to take in Aunt Celeste's hat. Some openly smirked. Grandmas clutched their pearls and frowned in disapproval.

Not that I blamed them. I half expected the thing to take flight at any moment myself and start fluttering around the rafters.

Once we were back in the car, Aunt Celeste finally unleashed her annoyance. "Those hypocritical. Little. Ninnies," she growled, jamming her seatbelt until it clicked. She took off the hat to wipe her forehead, and I realized I'd almost forgotten about her aqua hair. "Acting as though they've never seen a bit of formal headwear before. I swear, you try something new and different *one time*, and it's immediately a threat to humanity." She huffed and threw the car into reverse — "No class, I tell you." — and then into drive — "No class at all!"

The hatchback lurched, belched a cloud of black smoke, and then we were out of there, leaving God's House in the dust.

Despite her not-so-successful fashion moment, though, Aunt Celeste wasn't ready to leave Manhattan just yet. She insisted on taking me to lunch and wouldn't take no for an answer.

"How about Rudolfo's?" she asked. "They have the best soups in Midtown. Their French Onion?" — She puckered her lips and blew a chef's kiss — *"To die for."*

"Sounds great," I said.

It was a cloudy day in the city, which made the Christmas lights and window displays pop even more. We drifted up Sixth Avenue, horns blaring and pedestrians zigzagging everywhere with their latest purchases. Traffic slowed in front of Bryant Park, and as we sat idling for a moment, I could see people bundled up in coats and hats, their gloves wrapped around cups of that steaming hot chocolate I'd yet to get my hands—

"*OOF.*"

The dry-rotted seatbelt dug into my collarbone as we lurched forward again.

Aunt Celeste eased off the gas and lowered her chin sheepishly. "Sorry."

At some point we veered down a smaller side street, and the déjà vu got real. Every building and sign looked strangely familiar. We passed an abandoned church wedged between two apartment buildings, and I definitely remembered Clue mentioning how much she'd love to get her hands on it and repurpose the whole thing into a bed and breakfast or something.

And then it all made sense.

"Java the Hut!" I said, pointing across the intersection. "That's where Clue works."

"Jama the *who*?" Aunt Celeste squinted like she was an eighty-year-old trying to read one of those tiny subway line maps.

"Java the Hut. One of my" — I paused, not exactly sure I'd define Clue Perez as a friend — "one of those people I hung out with yesterday. She works at that coffee shop."

"Ohhh," Aunt Celeste said suspiciously, like she was on to something big. I looked over my shoulder and found her wiggling her eyebrows like a maniac. *"She."*

I turned back to the window without commenting. But as the old hatchback crept past the alley behind Java the Hut, my heart began racing. Because something was very, very wrong. A dump truck — the kind that Clue swore only came twice a month — was parked in the alley, its metal mouth open wide.

And it was devouring every single bag of trash from the Java the Hut dumpster.

CHAPTER 15

My mind went into overdrive. I snatched the radio, which I'd been instructed by Clue not to go anywhere without, from off the dashboard and fumbled over the door handle.

"Stop the car!" I yelled.

But the hatchback carried on.

"Nate, what on earth —?"

"Please," I said, half my body already leaning out the open door, "just stop!"

"Nate!"

Aunt Celeste slammed on the brakes, and I practically tumbled onto the sidewalk. By the time I reached the alley, the dump truck had already pulled away and was revving up the street.

"Wait!" I waved my arms frantically, but the workers didn't notice me in their mirrors, so I did the only other thing I could think of.

I ran.

I ran like my life depended on it, because, in a way, it sort of did. If those spikes got lost or fell into the wrong hands, we'd be in some serious doo-doo. My Chucks pounded the pavement, and my coat flapped behind me like a cape.

Everything hinged on that moment. If the truck turned onto the main road, into that sea of chaos, it was game over.

The icy air stung my eyes, but I kept blinking, kept running. I was so close…only a few feet more…. I pushed as hard as I could. My throat and chest were on fire, but I pushed. My calves felt like they were ripping apart, but I pushed. The back of the dump truck was right there, but it was picking up speed with every passing second.

I was so close. Just another inch or two.

Still running, I held out an arm as far as I could. My fingers stretched and stretched. Almost —

GOTCHA.

My fingers found metal, and after wrenching myself up onto the grimy ledge, I squeezed the button on the radio with my free hand. "Hello?" I panted. "Clue? Rodney?" I heaved another breath. *"Somebody!"*

The truck bounced along like a rickety, old rollercoaster, and the stench was horrendous. But I held on tight. Finally, the radio crackled, and Clue's voice broke through the static.

"Nate? What's wrong?"

"A dump truck," I managed. "A dump truck got the trash."

"*What*?! Don't let it get away!"

I swallowed, finally catching my breath again. "I'm not," I said. "I'm riding it right now!"

"Wait — really?" She almost sounded impressed.

"Yes, really," I gasped. "Okay. I'm going in."

Yeah.

Even I don't know what possessed me to say that. *I'm going in.* Like I was James Bond on a secret mission or something. But there it was in all its glory, the trash piled so high and so thick that the dump truck doors wouldn't even close all the way. Just waiting to swallow me up.

The whole thing reeked like sewage, but I didn't have time for second-guessing. I'd already told Clue I was handling it. So, I took the same approach I always used when getting into a chilly pool — I dove right in.

My entire body sank between the slick garbage bags. Mysterious juices oozed from every bag and plastic container, soaking my entire left sock not even five seconds in. And Clue wasn't kidding about the spoiled milk; it smelled like an animal had curled up and died. I dug as fast as I could, pushing aside discarded food cartons and tearing open any bag that felt like it might contain two spikes from the Rockefeller Center Christmas Tree star.

VrrOOMM.

The driver mashed the gas, and the truck swerved violently to the left. Before I could catch myself, my knees landed in a mound of soggy cardboard, and my elbow collided with something hard, sending my funny bone into a throbbing mess.

Wait a second....

Gritting my teeth through the discomfort, I tore open the bag lying under my elbow — and there they were. The ultimate dumpster dive find. The buried treasure I'd gone waist-deep in old ramen for.

There were the spikes, shimmering silver and crystal just like we'd left them.

CHAPTER 16

I waited until the truck made its next stop, and then I was out of there, scrambling over boxes and bags and jumping down onto the pavement before either of the workers noticed.

"Nate?"

I'd taken all of ten steps when her voice reached me. I lifted my head, and just as I caught sight of Clue jogging up the sidewalk, a glob of something brownish yellow dripped from my hair. A hand immediately went to her mouth, and I knew I must've looked like some kind of swamp monster.

"What...the *heck*," she gasped, clearly trying not to smile. "Are you okay?"

I closed my eyes and held up the bag of spikes. "Just peachy."

"Oh my gosh, are you kidding me?" The excitement in her voice didn't even sound like Clue. And then, from out of nowhere, she went in for a hug. "Oh — I..." She stopped short, lowering her arms and brushing the whole thing off. "Thank you," she said. "You have no idea how much trouble you just saved us."

"Mmm, I kind of do." I did my best to fling a patch of gummy broccoli from my sleeve. "So, what are you even doing here? It's Sunday."

She was wearing a black Java the Hut T-shirt, even though it was all of forty degrees outside.

"Right. Yeah, I'm covering a shift for Arlington." She pointed back to the coffee shop. "But I jetted as soon as you called."

Then came Aunt Celeste's voice — *"Nate?"* — followed by a closing car door. She'd pulled over and was standing in front of the hatchback, hands on her hips. But she didn't look angry. Just confused.

"I'd better go," I told Clue.

"Anddd I'll take these," she said, reaching for the spikes.

"You sure? They're a little heavy."

And just like that, in the span of two seconds, her whole demeanor returned to Old Clue. "Are you implying that I can't carry these?"

"No, I'm just saying —"

She grabbed the bag and heaved it over her shoulder. "Just make sure you're at the tree by seven, okay?"

"You're welcome!" I called as she walked away, still pulling food from my hair.

I'd barely buckled my seatbelt before the questions started firing.

"Nate, what's going on?" asked Aunt Celeste. "Why in the *world* did you go chasing after some dump truck? And why did you give that girl a bag of trash?"

At that point my brain was mushier than the garbage I'd just swam in, but I had to come up with something. "Sheee…justtt…really hates seeing so much go to landfills, you know? She's really eco-friendly that way."

Aunt Celeste shook her head. "Just when you think this city can't get any weirder." She started pulling away from the curb but suddenly tapped the brakes. "By the way," she added, scrunching her nose, "you have *got* to take a shower when we get home."

CHAPTER 17

A hush fell over the air, turning the night still and quiet — if only Jonah's heart was as calm. He stood there, alone in the dark alley, heart pounding inside his chest like a runaway drum.

THERE. There it was again, a scratching sound coming from beneath the pile of garbage bags stacked against the alley's brick wall.

Jonah flinched at the sound. But instead of running, he stayed. Instead of running, he moved closer. *He stood over the inky mess and, after swallowing his fear, even reached a shaking hand toward the one bag illuminated by a sliver of moonlight. His fingers twitched and quivered, but still he kept reaching. Finally, with a fistful of plastic, he lifted the bag —*

HSSSSS! Suddenly, a rat the size of Rhode Island pounced from the pavement and —

"This is ridiculous."

I slapped the notebook shut and stood. I was outside on Aunt Celeste's cramped balcony, relaxing among her potted assortment of dead ferns and vines, trying to enjoy the last few rays of daylight. For some crazy reason, I thought watching the orange sun sink behind the distant Manhattan skyline would somehow inspire me.

But there I was, writing a stupid story about trash and giant New York City rats. So that was a bust.

Around 6:15 p.m. I told Aunt Celeste and Gerdy goodbye (the two of them were curled up on the sofa with a tub of popcorn, about to watch some cheesy rom-com) and then headed to the subway station on 36th. I had about thirty minutes to kill on the train, so I kept my head down and buried myself in my notebook again.

The train rattled and swayed, but no matter what direction it took, it failed to jostle any sort of inspiration. I used to be able to write at the drop of a hat — everything from zombie invasions to murder mysteries to talking animals with magical powers (that was a weird phase). But my mind had been drawing a lot of blanks lately, like all the words and ideas and creativity had dried up. The thing was, I could pinpoint the exact moment the drought started.

When McKenna and I parted ways, something happened. A lightbulb dimmed. A spark sputtered out. It was as if a piece of me or a piece of my talent — which I was beginning to doubt ever existed in the first place — left with her.

I don't know. Maybe I was just sad about the whole thing, about the way it all ended.

"Good grief, if you miss her that much, just write her a sappy love letter."

Clue's voice trumped every other noise in the subway car. My eyes jumped from the empty page and immediately connected with hers. She had walked to the same station, gotten on the same train, and been sitting directly across from me the entire time.

"Wha —" My mouth was just as dry as my creativity. "What are you doing here?"

Clue crossed her arms and leaned back in the seat. Her eyes narrowed beneath the brim of her black beanie. "You know, if I didn't have such a remarkably thick skin, I'd be a little offended that you keep asking me that."

"Sorry. I just...I wasn't expecting to see you. I didn't know you lived in Sunset."

"All my life." Clue nodded to the notebook in my lap. "Now, how about that love letter."

I rolled my eyes and shifted uncomfortably. "I'm not writing a letter. I'm just...thinking."

"Maybe you weren't *planning* to, but judging by that pitiful look on your face, I'd say you *need* to." She shrugged. "Something's eating you up."

As much as I hated to admit it, she was right. To an extent. I needed to write McKenna, not a gushy love letter or anything, but I needed to get some weight off my chest. She was with someone new, and if that's what she wanted, then okay. Was I under the impression that she liked me as much as I liked her? Yes. Did I hope we'd start dating soon? Maybe go to the spring dance together? Possibly.

But I couldn't keep moping around forever. It had been over two months, so I needed to do *something*, for my own sanity if for nothing else.

Clue wasn't looking anymore. She was busy blowing bubbles with her gum and musing over some old man in the corner who was making a video with a Chucky doll. Most everyone else was watching too, so it felt like I finally had the breathing space to write.

Dear McKenna,

You'll never see this letter, but that's the point. I'm not doing it for you. I'm doing it for me.

The first thing you should hypothetically know is that I'm not mad. Maybe I was for a while, but I've learned that being mad doesn't change or solve anything. It only makes you miserable. And I'm done feeling miserable.

The second thing is that while I may not be mad, I am confused. I'm still so confused about what happened to us. Do you even know? Here's the last thing I remember: We were planning on seeing that new movie — Nothing, Nothing — and then we never did. Turns out, you went with Travis instead. Did you know that I knew that?

I think that's when everything changed. We just stopped hanging out. We stopped texting. We stopped those late-night story times. Remember those? We'd lie in our beds and I'd call you and you'd ask me to read something over the phone from my latest story. You said you could listen to me for hours.

But then we stopped. And the thing is, I don't even know if you noticed, because nothing was ever said. No explanation. No halfhearted excuse.

One moment we were…and then we weren't.

Now it's time for the last thing. I'd be lying if I said I didn't miss you. I'd be lying if I said it didn't still hurt when I see you with someone else. But I can't keep missing and hurting and feeling all those things. You didn't want me or choose me, so I have to find a way to move on, just like you've done.

That's why the last thing is goodbye.

Goodbye, McKenna. Thank you for the coffee dates, the Harry Potter *movie nights, the hikes, and every laugh in between. I wish you could've been happy with me.*

— Nate

CHAPTER 18

"Okay, cough it up."

"What?"

I was still cleaning the teardrops from my glasses when Clue's grabby hands reached across the train car.

"Come on, Farm Boy. Don't be shy," she said, snatching the book from my fingers. I tried to save it, but she was already out of reach. "Relaaax. I won't read a thing."

My stomach twisted into a hundred knots, but I wasn't about to stand up and cause a scene on the subway. Clue knew that.

She leaned against a metal pole, casually flipping to the page I'd just poured my heart out on. Then, without saying a word, she ripped the page right out and tossed the notebook back to me.

"Hey —" I tried. But Clue ignored me.

She folded the letter in half and held it up for me to see, like she was a model for *The Price Is Right.*

"I'm doing you a favor," she said, walking over to the set of sliding doors. "Trust me. If you keep this, you'll be too tempted to look at it. And then you'll be crying all over again."

A wave of heat shot up my neck and into my cheeks. I guess she'd seen the tears. "Fine. So, now what?"

"Please hold."

Clue slipped the letter into the seam where the two silver train doors met, where there was somehow just enough of a crack to break through. But she didn't let go; she kept the note pinched between two fingers. As the train sped on, the paper flapped wildly outside the car, like a white baby bird trying to take flight.

"Ready?" she asked.

I glanced around the train car, but nobody was paying us a speck of attention. I nodded.

"Say goodbye to all that negativity in three...two...*one*...."

She released the letter. The rushing air immediately sucked it outside the subway, and there it went, swirling away, floating past the windows.

My goodbye.

Lost in the tunnels forever.

The subway eventually spit us out near Rockefeller Center. As we climbed the stairs and emerged from underground, Rodney's muffled voice started crackling through our radios.

"'evening, mates," he said.

"Hey, Rodney, what's u—" My insides lurched as Clue suddenly yanked me aside to avoid being trampled by a mob of tourists racing to catch their own train.

But my body never stopped. My feet lost traction and somehow got tangled up with Clue's clunky boots. We wobbled and skidded until we finally came crashing down onto the sidewalk together, me on top of her.

We lay there for what seemed like an eternity, both of us too stunned to speak. Horns continued to honk, sirens continued to blare, and people continued to ebb and flow all around. The city never stopped, but for those few brief seconds, as our breath hung in the icy air, it's as if time stood still between us.

Our faces were inches apart, so all I could do was stare into her big, beautiful brown eyes while my brain tried its best to restart.

"Hellooo?"

Rodney.

My hand was still clenched around the radio. Groaning, I quickly hoisted myself up, careful not to knee Clue in the stomach. I offered her a hand, but of course she refused.

"Rodney," I said a bit disoriented. My mind still hung up on Clue's eyes and perfectly smooth lips. "Hey. Sorry about that."

"I'm with the heavenly hosts," Rodney continued proudly. "I repeat, *I'm with the heavenly hosts.*"

"Heavenly hosts" — Rodney's apparent codename for the dozen white-wire angels playing their trumpets along the Channel Gardens. We found him there in the hazy glow, halfway in a bush and bent over awkwardly with his camera, trying his best to capture the perfect shot.

Clue marched over and slapped him on the thigh with the back of her hand. "Yo. Let's go."

Startled, Rodney faceplanted right into the shrubbery. I helped him up as Clue turned and headed for the tree.

Shady Springs is a one-stoplight town, which meant the three of us — dressed in all black like a bunch of ninjas and toting around big black backpacks at night — would definitely attract some unwanted attention. But this was New York City. We were some of the *least* suspicious-looking people, which meant we weaved through the crowd almost invisibly.

"What, no smoke bombs?"

We were standing near the tree, but from what I observed, nothing was happening. Some beefy dude who'd just gotten a hotdog from a nearby weenie stand was yelling at the poor guy selling them, demanding a refund because he'd received sweet relish instead of spicy. But other than that, the place was pretty calm. No explosions or giant puffs of smoke anywhere.

"Of course not," said Clue, taking her jacket off and tying it around her waist. She'd roasted in the tree last night too. "What's the fun in using the same diversion twice?"

She shared a knowing smirk with Rodney, and just when I was about to ask what was going on, I got my answer.

Suddenly, the biggest baby kangaroo I've ever seen in my entire life emerged — no, *floated* — from around the corner of 30 Rock. The thing was the size of a blimp and looked absolutely ridiculous. Its chubby thighs were stuffed in a blowup diaper, and it was sucking on a baby blue pacifier. Oh, and I can't forget the frilly bonnet tied around its ears. That completed the ensemble.

As the enormous joey drifted closer, I couldn't help but imagine Gerdy as a float. Something about the diaper, I think.

"What is that thing?"

"Kangaroo Kid, of course," said Rodney. "He's sort of the mascot for Mum's magazine, so every year they enter him in the Macy's Thanksgiving Day Parade."

"Okay...but what's he doing here now?"

"He's tonight's diversion, mate!" said Rodney, squinting with one eye and aiming his camera high. He grabbed the shot and then let the camera dangle loosely around his neck again. "It was pretty easy too. Just whipped out a few Benjamins, asked some of Mum's assistants to take the little rugrat out for another spin, and here we are!"

Crazy or not, the float worked. People gasped and pointed and moved toward it with cameras rolling. Their flashes lit up the joey's big underbelly like a brown thunderstorm.

"Okay, people, let's *move*."

In a nanosecond, Clue was under the tree and swinging up to the lowest branches, as if they were a set of monkey bars.

CHAPTER 19

We seemed to reach the top faster that night. Maybe we were better prepared for the claustrophobic heat, or maybe we had unknowingly learned a thing or two about climbing ridiculously huge Christmas trees since our first attempt, I don't know.

Whatever the reason, I wasn't complaining. The sooner we started, the sooner we could get the heck out of there.

"Okay," said Clue. She was already elbow-deep in her backpack. "If you can hold off on the diary entries for, like, at least the next couple of hours or so, that'd be great."

We were sitting on opposite sides of the star again. She peeked around the sculpture, but instead of giving me her signature death glare, like I was the most annoying person on the planet, she *grinned*.

I mean, it was objectively the tiniest grin in the history of grins. More like a spasm really. At first I thought maybe it was just a twisting shadow playing tricks with my eyes. But no, Clue definitely smiled.

"What?" she said.

I must've been staring too hard for too long.

"Huh? Oh. Nothing, I —" I reeled my neck back in and blinked about a dozen times while Clue snapped her goggles in place. "I'll try to control myself."

The three of us had our routine down to a T. Clue was an expert with the blowtorch, carefully slicing off one spike at a time. I'd gotten pretty quick with grabbing and releasing spikes down the tree. And Rodney, judging by how fast he returned the canvas bag, was stuffing those spikes into his backpack like a champ.

Unfortunately, he could only stuff two. Those suckers were a good fifteen pounds apiece and almost two feet long, so our bags couldn't hold much more than that. Neither could our spines.

So, instead of lowering the third spike down with the rope, I shrugged off my own backpack, shoved the spike inside, and then hung it on a nearby branch.

By eight-thirty, Clue had started working away on the fourth spike of the night. The wind picked up, which made the tree a little more wobbly than usual, but we steadied ourselves by squeezing our knees tighter around the branches we sat on and plowed ahead. A constant flicker of light reflected in Clue's goggles, almost like a mini strobe light, as she slowly traced her flame around the spike's steel base.

But then it happened. The one thing I was worried about.

A rogue spark escaped, and instead of burning out like the others, it drifted onto a branch a few feet below us. It lay there, hot and golden. *Simmering*.

"Clue." I pointed, and she looked.

"Uhh, not good," she said, extinguishing her flame and taking off her goggles. "Really, *really* not good."

It was the first time I'd heard a hint of uncertainty in her voice, but she had every right to be nervous. The spark was still glowing, and the patch of needles it had landed on was starting to smolder. A whisp of smoke curled upward.

"Wait —"

I wrenched my water bottle from my backpack, leaned over as far as I could, and began pouring. Half the bottle emptied before my aim zeroed in and actually hit the target.

Tsssss!

We both heaved a sigh of relief as the fiery-red needles turned to ash.

Crisis averted.

But I must've relaxed too much, or lost my focus, because the next thing I knew, my hand slipped — and suddenly I was falling.

CHAPTER 20

My stomach slid into my throat as I dropped.

"Nate!"

Clue's voice echoed after me, but she was too far away to actually do anything. All I could do was let gravity take me, needles and twigs slapping my face relentlessly as I fell. I kept blinking so I didn't get stabbed in the eyes.

And then, somehow, by the grace of God, my fingers caught a sturdy branch.

"Errr..." I couldn't help but grit my teeth and groan as my arms struggled to hold me up. I wasn't the fittest sixteen-year-old dude. Instead of spending hours at the gym, I was usually huddled in the corner of a coffee shop somewhere with my notebook. But in that moment, as I hung suspended like a one hundred fifty-pound icicle with minimal upper-body strength, I really started to regret that decision.

Finally, my feet found some sort of landing. My shoulders felt like two knotted fireballs, but after a few minutes of struggling, I somehow managed to claw my way back up to the star.

"Are you *trying* to give me a heart attack?" Clue looked like she was about to throw me out of the tree herself.

I massaged one of my shoulders. "Not exactly," I said, wincing.

Chest and stomach still quivering, I could've easily puked right then and there. A nice surprise for Rodney down below.

Clue stared at me for the longest time, her eyes practically bulging in the star's crystal reflection. She seemed angry, terrified, and relieved all at once.

"Should we stop?" she asked, and I could tell from her voice and concerned expression that she really meant it. "I don't want you dying on me or anything."

She was already halfway through the fourth spike, and apparently the infamous Miss Mable would be leaving Clue's apartment by 10 p.m. again, so we decided to finish that one and head out.

I tried putting it in my backpack, but of course Clue insisted that she take it, that way we'd each have only one spike to handle coming down.

As soon as Rodney gave the signal that the coast was clear, we hopped off from the last branches and onto the pavement.

"Great," he said, after we'd put some distance between us and the tree. "Let's stash these beauts with the others that Nate saved this morning and be on our way." He wriggled his shoulders and adjusted the straps of his backpack; I'd almost forgotten that he was carrying two spikes. "Where did you hide them? Hopefully not in another garbage bin," he said with a laugh.

Clue tugged at her beanie, pulling it over her ears even more. She looked off in the distance and squinted. "My place."

Rodney's mouth froze wide open. He looked like he wanted to laugh again. "*Your* place," he said. "You're joking. You took them to your apartment?"

"I didn't know what else to do, okay?" said Clue, finally looking him in the eye. "It was broad daylight. I had to stash them somewhere."

"Yes, but dragging them to Brooklyn doesn't exactly fit into the whole 'save the day' angle you're going for. I mean, are you just supposed to be in complete shock that they're in your apartment?" Rodney threw on a fake, high-pitched voice that sort of reminded me of Aunt Celeste's old audition tapes she used to post on YouTube. "Oh, dear, how did *those* get in here? I had *no* idea these giant, disassembled pieces of the Rockefeller Center Christmas Tree star were hiding in my closet. It wasn't me, officers!"

"Okay." I had to say something. Rodney was going over the top, even by Rodney standards, and his dramatic monologue wasn't getting us anywhere. Plus, it was freezing. "Let's just get over there, grab the other spikes, and figure out what to do with them."

"Good idea. Thank you, *Nate*," said Clue. She gave Rodney a dark look, and then we all headed to the subway station.

CHAPTER 21

"You know you don't have to schlep all the way to Brooklyn, right?"

"Are you joking?" Rodney took off his beanie, letting that blonde hair fly, and proudly held it up to his chest like a pledge. "A soldier *never* leaves his troop behind!" And then he shrugged. "Plus, Mum's hosting a stupid holiday party for some colleagues. I reckon this is my chance to miss the whole thing."

We were back on the train, rattling our way across the East River. I sat glued to my notebook, and Clue and Rodney were back to being...well...Clue and Rodney. It was hard to keep up with their rollercoaster of a friendship.

But the closer we got to Sunset Park, the quieter Clue became. In fact, she didn't say another word for the remainder of the ride over. We climbed out of the subway on 36th, passed through the neon glow of a string of crummy delis and convenience stores, dragged our backpacks another couple of blocks, and then finally arrived at Clue's apartment.

"Fair warning," she said, breaking her twenty-minute silent streak. "It's a bit of a mess."

She led us up three flights of rickety stairs. I imagined the wood was beautiful in its heyday, before its deep, rich hue was covered in scratches and paint splatters. Clue pointed out Miss Mable's apartment on our way up. Her door was the same slab of peeling red as all the others.

We stopped at apartment thirteen. Both numbers had lost their golden sheen, and the door's chipped paint revealed a rainbow of colors from years past. Clue began fishing the key from her pocket.

"Sorry again for the mess," she said. "I didn't have time to wash the dishes in the sink. And I'm pretty sure I've still got a load of laundry on the —"

"Clue," I said, "it's all good. Seriously, you should see my aunt's place. It's nothing but costumes and shredded goat toys everywhere."

"Not to interrupt," said Rodney, interrupting, "but does anyone else smell something burning?"

Clue and I glanced at him, then each other, as our noses went to work. Rodney was right. There was a smokiness to the air, like someone had just blown out their birthday candles.

And it was growing stronger by the second.

Clue quickly unlocked the door and threw it open. *"Mom?"*

We all rushed inside, but the first thing I noticed wasn't the stack of dirty dishes in the sink or the basket of laundry on the dining room table.

The first thing I noticed when entering Clue's apartment was the cloud of thick gray smoke.

CHAPTER 22

The fire alarm started beeping just as everyone sprang into action. Clue ran to the kitchen, where a thin woman was pacing around in a cream nightgown, and Rodney and I dove into the living room to crack open every window we could.

"Mom, what are doing?" said Clue, turning knobs and throwing open the oven door.

Coughing, she pulled out whatever charred debris was in there, tossed the pan onto the stovetop with a loud *clank*, and started fanning the fire alarm with a hand towel. The beeping eventually stopped — but the commotion didn't seem to have the slightest effect on Clue's mom. She just stood there in the corner of the kitchen, arms slightly raised, rocking from one foot to the other. Her wide eyes continued blinking, but she seemed so far away. Part of me wondered if she'd been sleepwalking.

"Mom," said Clue, crossing the hazy kitchen, "what's going on? What happened?"

Clue spoke gently now, almost motherly. Her mom, on the other hand, struggled to find words. "I — I tried making toast," she said groggily, "but the oven —" She pointed. "I couldn't turn it off."

Making toast must've been a whole ordeal because every inch of counter space was covered in slices of bread, smears of butter, and wads of napkins.

"Then why didn't you take out the bread?"

Clue's mom just kept on blinking.

"Here," said Clue. She wrapped her arms around her mom and pulled her in close. The woman looked so small and frail compared to her, but maybe it was just the nightgown and messy hair giving her a somewhat sickly appearance.

"I'm sorry," said the woman, her voice muffled in Clue's shoulder. "I'm sorry."

"Ssh, it's okay." Clue tucked some of her mom's hair behind her ear. "But you aren't supposed to be fooling with the stove, remember? Especially after Miss Mable leaves."

The woman nodded and stood straight again. For the first time, she turned and noticed Rodney and me. We probably looked like two robbers, waiting in the dim glow of the entryway with our black jeans, coats, and hats.

Rodney waved. "Hello, Miss P."

Clue's mom lifted a hand and said, "Hi, Rodney. Good to see you." And then she looked at me expectantly, almost like a child waiting for a piece of candy.

"It's nice to meet you, Mrs. Perez," I said, stepping forward. I shook her outstretched hand as gently as possible. "I'm Nate. Clue and Rodney's friend."

The word *friend* tasted funny as it spilled out of my mouth, but it was the only thing that made sense. I could've gone with *heist buddy* or *fellow criminal*, but I guess I was still in denial.

"Hi, Nate. I'm so glad you could come over," said Mrs. Perez, as if the whole thing were nothing more than a quiet game night we'd been planning for weeks. As if she hadn't almost burned the entire apartment building to the ground. She kept my hand clasped between hers.

I looked at Clue, and she nodded, giving me the go-ahead. "I tell you what, why don't we go sit on the couch while they clean up some. Is that okay?" I looped her arm through mine, and the two of us shuffled over to the living room so Clue and Rodney could focus on the kitchen.

Mrs. Perez didn't say much, but when she did, it was usually about Clue. Things like "She's such a strong girl." Or "There's my lovely girl." Or "I don't know what I'd do without my special girl." Clue would glance over occasionally, and I'd just nod and grin, letting her know it was all good. After piecing the kitchen back together, she came over and announced it was time for her mom to get back to bed.

"Nice meeting you …" Mrs. Perez's voice trailed off as she shuffled back to her bedroom. She stopped and turned.

"Nate," I reminded her.

"Yes," she said, jabbing a finger skyward. "Nate. Goodnight."

CHAPTER 23

Rodney and I sat in silence while Clue disappeared to help her mom get settled. Me on one side of the lumpy couch, him on the other. Neither of us said a word for the longest time. I mean, I didn't exactly know *what* to say. Everything had happened so fast, a whirlwind of smoke and anxiety and burnt toast. Now that things had subsided, though, the apartment was eerily quiet. Even the sirens seemed to have taken a break.

Looking around, I noticed there were no overhead lights in Clue's apartment, only a few lamps scattered around on side tables and one in the corner. Wood paneling from at least fifty years ago covered the walls. I ran my Converses over the thick mustard-yellow carpet. Or maybe orange?

It was hard to tell in the gloom.

"They can barely afford to keep the lights on, mate."

I turned at the sound of Rodney's voice.

"Clue and Miss P.," he said, keeping his voice low. He started chewing the inside of his cheek and shifted on the couch cushion. "That's why Clue doesn't have a cellphone. That's why she works so hard to earn a little extra money." He looked around the room, shaking his head. "Miss P. gets a pension from her old nursing job, of course, but it can't be much."

"She's retired?"

Mrs. Perez couldn't be a day over fifty.

"She had to, mate." Rodney stared at the carpet, sighing. "Miss P.'s got what they call early-onset dementia. It came out of nowhere, really. She'd forget her route to work and wind up taking wrong trains. One day she went missing for *hours*. They finally found her up in the Bronx, wandering around Yankee Stadium." Rodney took another deep breath. "I know it's not my place to say…but I figured your brain's got about a million questions right now."

I nodded, still processing.

I'd been so determined to learn Clue's story, to uncover the big mystery of Cluenette Perez, that I hadn't stopped to consider what that mystery might actually be. Now that I knew some of the truth, I didn't know what to think. I didn't know what to do with all that information.

I just wanted Clue and her mom to be okay.

"She made me swear not to tell anyone," Rodney added. "Especially my parents."

I put my hands up. "I'm not saying a word. Promise."

"Promise what?"

Clue emerged from the dark hallway and plopped down in the chair next to Rodney's end of the sofa. Rodney and I exchanged looks, and judging by the momentary silence, I knew he was scrambling for an answer too.

"I...promised Rodney that I would teach him how to milk a cow one day," I said. Rodney nodded in agreement. "You know, because I'm a Farm Boy from Virginia and all that."

Clue narrowed her eyes. "You two are so weird."

"How is she?" Rodney asked.

Clue curled up in the armchair. "She's okay. Just tired and a little confused." She picked at a loose thread on the knee of her black overalls, the other arm propping up her head. Clue sighed. And then, when she was good and ready, she whispered, "She's getting worse."

Rodney leaned forward, elbows on his knees. "I know she is," he said. "But it's like I told you. I can ask my parents if they would —"

"No," said Clue, pulling her hand away from her ear and sitting up straighter. "I already told you I'm not begging your parents to take in me and my sick mom."

"It wouldn't be begging, C. And you said so yourself she's getting worse. I don't think it's safe for her to be alone anymore, especially since —"

Suddenly, Clue sprang from the chair.

"Don't you think I know that?" she snapped. "I'm terrified every time I walk out that door," she

said, pointing. "That she's gonna find the kitchen knives. Or run a bath too hot. Or open up the front door and just disappear forever."

Her voice shook. And for the first time, I saw true tears in Clue's eyes. Tears I didn't think were possible.

"I'm terrified every single day," she croaked, before slumping into the chair again. "But I don't know what else to do."

She blinked, and in no time, the tears disappeared.

As if they hadn't been there at all.

CHAPTER 24

My MetroCard was getting a serious workout, because for the third time that night, I was back on the subway and crossing the Manhattan Bridge. We'd grabbed the spikes that Clue had hidden under her bed, so now we each had two stuffed in our backpacks.

"Glad to see we're all sharing the load this time," Rodney teased, eyebrows raised.

For it to be so late, the train was pretty crowded, and seats were limited. I had no choice but to squeeze in between Clue and some hulk-sized dude in a gray tracksuit. He kept his hood up, but I imagined a green face and thick unibrow somewhere underneath. Rodney took an empty seat across from us.

As he snapped photos and chatted with every stranger within spitting distance, Clue and I sat quietly. I would've made small talk about the weather or her college plans — or even whipped out my notebook — but all I could focus on were our shoulders smooshed together. Not that we had any other choice. The train was packed, but still.

I wondered if she noticed our shoulders too.

"Thanks for that back there."

Clue was the first to speak, but she wasn't looking at me. She was playing with her fingers in her lap, which was strange, because Clue wasn't the type to twiddle her thumbs.

"Of course," I said. "Your mom seems like a really nice lady."

Clue smiled, still picking at her nails. "She is. She's a little forgetful sometimes, but uh…" Her jaw went rigid as her voice caught in her throat. She quickly wiped under her eye before speaking again. "But she's the best."

As the train raced ahead at lightning speed, and as the warmth between our shoulders grew, I wanted nothing more than to squeeze Clue's hand. I wanted to pry it loose from all the fidgeting and just comfort her in some way.

But I knew she'd slap me if I did. One hundred percent.

Clue and Rodney knew the subway like the back of their hands. Good thing too, because if I were navigating it on my own, I probably would've ended up somewhere in Queens. Every time the train stopped, I made a move to stand, only to have Clue yank me back down by the elbow. "Not yet," she kept saying.

We rode the train all the way to Central Park, so by the time we climbed the stairs, trees were towering above us instead of skyscrapers. Instead of lush green, though, everything was pitch-black — which was the whole point.

"You need a public enough space where anyone could've hidden the star, right?" Rodney had said before we left the apartment. "*And* you need it to be somewhat dark, so no one sees the dirty deed. It's perfect!"

I'd never been to Central Park, but I imagined it was less creepy during the day. (Again, way too much true crime.) It could've done with a few more lampposts in my opinion, but like I said,

Clue and Rodney were the experts. We were headed to some place called the Cop Cot. I'd googled it on the train, and from what I could gather, it was a wooden rotunda made up of twisted branches and leafy vines. Like something you'd find in the elvish kingdom of Rivendell.

Which, when I thought about it, was probably why Clue and Rodney said they used to play there as kids.

As we made our way along the winding path, I knew it was going to be a better hiding spot than the coffee shop dumpster. Not only was there zero chance of a trash pickup interference, but the place was almost completely deserted. We passed a couple of late-night runners and a woman walking her chubby bulldog, and that was it.

The rotunda was just like the pictures online — only a little less magical. Instead of the leaves and fresh flowers of summer, the domed ceiling was now a canopy of brown, withered vines. Wooden benches lined the hexagon structure, but Google had failed to mention the Styrofoam cups, straws, and plastic candy wrappers left behind by visitors.

Rodney stepped inside the rotunda first and began scanning the floor as he went. He moved slowly and deliberately, tapping along with the toe of his boot, like he was cranking out Morse code or something. Clue and I kept a lookout for passersby.

Suddenly, Rodney's breath caught in his throat. He tapped some more.

"Yes!" he whispered excitedly. "I think it's still here!"

He set his backpack down, dropped to his knees, and began pulling on one of the large slate tiles. The grout was long gone, so he was able to wedge his fingers into the groove, pick up, and slide the tile across the floor.

Clue and I rushed to his side. "I don't believe it," she said. "I thought they would've patched this up years ago."

We were looking into a dark hole where the tile had been moments before. It was over a foot wide and who knew how deep. Deep enough to hold the spikes at least, because Rodney began unpacking his and dumping them into the hole.

"Remember that time we hid our Halloween candy in here?" he asked Clue. "We came back a week later, and the bugs had ruined it all."

"Yeah," said Clue, kneeling with her own backpack. "Not our finest hour."

She unloaded her spikes, and then it was my turn. I knelt beside them and peered into the hole, imagining a tribe of beetles devouring fun-sized Snickers and Tootsie Rolls oozing with worms. I unzipped my bag, reached inside — and my heart immediately dropped.

Clue must've noticed. "What is it?" she said. "What's wrong?"

I swallowed, and for a split second, I thought about lying. But it was no use.

They had to know. And I'd just have to deal with the consequences.

"This isn't my bag."

CHAPTER 25

"Ha ha. Very funny."

Clue gave me that infamous look of hers, the one where she just stared at me, unfazed, and waited until I gave up on the joke.

"I'm serious," I said. "This isn't the backpack we got from Rodney's dad. I mean, it *looks* like it, but it's different. It's filled with..." My fingers wrapped around the first thing I found. It was cool to the touch, and when I pulled it out of the bag, we all found ourselves staring at —

"Are those nunchucks?" asked Rodney.

I tossed the nunchucks onto the stone floor, reached back into the bag, and pulled out...a metal hammer. And then a tiny spear. Then an axe. Then a scythe. Then a knife.

Clue snatched the knife before I could toss it. "These are *weapons*," she said, carefully running a gloved finger along the blade. "I don't understand. When did this happen?"

"The train," Rodney said thoughtfully. We both looked at him. "The guy beside you had a backpack on the floor too.... I bet he grabbed yours when he got off!"

"Great," said Clue, tossing the knife into the bag. She stood and brushed off her pants. "Just great. We've switched bags with a serial killer."

Rodney finished dragging the tile back into place, and it was as if we had never been there. As if there weren't hundreds of thousands of dollars' worth of Christmas spirit hidden in the dirt. "Let's not jump to conclusions. Perhaps we can track them down somehow —"

"In New York?" said Clue. "Are you kidding? That bag could be anywhere by now. Forget it. It's over."

I couldn't help but think Clue was right. My backpack — the *real* one — might as well have been lost at sea. As we strapped on our bags and started snaking our way across the park, no one really said anything. No one was in the mood. If it weren't for the faint honking of horns outside the park and the *clack clack clack* of horse-drawn carriages, I'd almost have thought I was back in the quiet Virginian countryside.

As soon as we reached Gapstow Bridge, I recognized it immediately — and didn't even need Google to do so. *Home Alone 2* has always been one of my favorite movies. That moment when Kevin meets the homeless pigeon lady standing on the Pond's edge? Classic.

We'd been walking in silence for what seemed like an eternity, and deep down, I just knew Clue hated me. Why wouldn't she? My backpack was my responsibility, and I'd let it slip through my fingers. Clue's lips may have been sealed, but I was sure her mind was buzzing. Probably thinking of all the ways she could kill me.

Finally, Rodney broke the crushing silence. He asked Clue a question, but his words hung in the air unanswered. He and I had crossed the bridge. When we turned around, thinking Clue was still on our heels, we saw she had stopped in the middle of the bridge and was looking out over the Pond.

I was the first to jog over. When I reached her side, I followed her gaze and found that she was staring up at the Plaza Hotel, its twinkling lights reflected in the water below.

"We'll get them back, okay? I promise."

I hoped my words didn't sound empty.

"I admire your optimism, Farm Boy." (I decided to let that one slide, all things considered.) Clue sighed and shook her head. "Do you ever wish you could just skip ahead, like ten years into the future, and start living your dreams? Just time jump to that perfect career. To the things you always wanted."

Not once did she take her eyes off the Plaza, its ivory walls illuminated like a palace. But I knew there was more to her question than just architectural design aspirations. In my gut, I knew Clue was also thinking about her mom. Perhaps she was hoping and praying for a future where her mom wasn't sick…where she didn't have to constantly worry about her mom's wellbeing. A future where she could finally slow down, provide for the two of them, and make her mom as comfortable as possible.

That's what *I* would pray for.

"Sometimes," I admitted. "But then I wonder if we'd miss the dreaming part. You know? Those moments when your stomach is filled with butterflies and you fall asleep with a smile on your face, just thinking about all the possibilities." I shrugged and couldn't help but think about my writing. My own goals. "I think if you just landed in your dreams, maybe you wouldn't appreciate them as much."

Clue still didn't look at me. She kept her chin up and her eyes focused ahead, but a smile pulled at the corner of her lips. "You're like a walking fortune cookie, you know that?" She held her stance for a beat more, and when she finally turned to me, there were tears sparkling in her eyes. "Thanks," she whispered.

"ALRIGHT, MATES. *PICTURE TIME*!"

Rodney was now behind us, his camera already locked and loaded. "You two in front," he said. "The Plaza in the back."

Clue groaned in protest, but Rodney insisted. In order to get his perfect shot, he asked us to hop up on the bridge's stone ledge. I jumped up first and was surprised when Clue accepted my hand for help. The stone was a little slick with some kind of frozen moisture, so we slowly waddled an inch at a time until we were facing each other. With the Plaza between us, Rodney guided our cupped hands so they were situated under the hotel in his frame, that way it appeared like we were holding the Plaza up. Or delivering it to someone's doorstep.

"Oh, that's perfect, that is." Once satisfied, Rodney gave a thumbs up, peered into the viewfinder, and started counting. "One…two…*three*."

The flash went off like a burst of lightning, forcing me to blink in surprise.

But Clue did more than blink.

Startled, she staggered on the icy stone, and before I could grab her, she slipped right over the edge.

CHAPTER 26

I'll never forget her scream.

It echoed through the park, bouncing off the rocks and ricocheting against the trees. She seemed to fall in slow motion, but we still weren't fast enough; all we grabbed was air. Clue crashed into the slushie water below, sending a flock of bobbing ducks into a squawking, flapping frenzy.

Rodney and I raced down the grassy embankment. "Clue!" I yelled. "Hang on, we're coming!"

"She can't swim!" said Rodney, which only added to everyone's anxiety.

But he did think on his feet and quickly grabbed a dead tree branch nearby. We heaved it over to the Pond's edge and extended it as far as we could, close to where Clue was flailing and splashing.

"Grab on!" I shouted.

Coughing and sputtering, she flung her arms around the branch, and Rodney and I began pulling.

We dragged her through the water, and by the time she reached the bank, she was white as a sheet and cold as ice.

"We've got to get her indoors," said Rodney, as we hoisted Clue to her feet. We stood on either side so she could drape her arms over our shoulders. "Come on!"

By the time we climbed back up the hill, a white carriage carrying a couple of tourists was clacking toward us. I waved it down, and the coachman yanked back the reigns. His horse stopped immediately, blowing out a spray of spit and misty vapors.

"Please," I said breathlessly. "Our friend. She just fell in the water. Can you get us out of here?"

After helping Clue into the carriage, we fell into one of the red velvet seats. Two ladies, bundled up from head to toe, sat across from us.

"Bless her heart," said the brown-haired woman. "Here." She unfolded a thick blanket and passed it over. "You all must be freezing."

"Yes," said Rodney. "Thank you."

The blanket smelled like wet horse, but it was heavy and warm, so we quickly spread it across our legs as the lady continued: "I'm Debbie," she said, "and this is my sister Laura."

Laura smiled and held out a plastic bag. "Chestnut?"

Thankfully, Rodney's home was just outside the park. He gave the coachman his address, and after a swift and unanimous vote of support from Debbie and Laura, who seemed much more interested in our dilemma than finishing their carriage ride, we galloped down Fifth Avenue. I didn't know a horse-drawn carriage could travel so fast. We weaved through traffic like we had an engine of our own, and at one point, I'm pretty sure we popped a side wheelie to zoom in front of a taxi.

In less than a minute, we were on the curb and dragging Clue toward the front entrance of the Donoghue residence. A different doorman, who I assumed covered the night shift, greeted us as he held open the golden door.

"Everything all right, Mr. Donoghue?" He tried his best to smile, but I'm sure the sight of Clue, draped over us like a frozen zombie, was a cause for concern.

"It will be!" Rodney called back. "Thanks, Winslow!"

We rode the elevator up to the penthouse. As soon as the doors slid open, we staggered into the foyer and were greeted by a symphony of Christmas music, laughter, and the clinking of glasses. Mrs. Donoghue's party was still going strong.

"Mum!" said Rodney, speaking of Mrs. Donoghue.

She had just entered the foyer from a side hallway and was gliding across the marble floor with all the elegance of a queen. When she heard Rodney's voice over the music, though, she stopped dead in her tracks.

"Rodney?" She took one look at Clue, who was now trembling between us, and said, "What on earth is going on?"

CHAPTER 27

Mrs. Donoghue hiked up her long green dress and rushed over. She felt Clue's cheeks and forehead with the back of her jeweled hand while Rodney explained what had happened.

"It's nearly midnight," said Mrs. Donoghue. She kept her voice lowered, like she really thought her fancy guests could hear us over whatever obnoxious rendition of "Twelve Days of Christmas" was playing on the surround sound. "I thought you were upstairs in your room, not traipsing through Central Park. It's entirely too late, *and* it's a school night." She dug her cellphone out of some invisible pocket on her dress and started tapping the screen furiously. "I'm calling a taxi and taking this poor girl to the hospital before she —"

"No!"

The word left me before I even knew what was happening. Mrs. Donoghue and I were basically strangers; I'd been in her home once. We'd exchanged a few words over eggs Florentine and toast, and there I was practically shouting in her face.

Rodney came to the rescue. "She just needs to warm up a bit," he said. "Maybe drink something hot."

"She *needs* some dry clothes," said Mrs. Donoghue.

Which was true. A puddle of water had started to form around Clue's boots, slowing spreading out across the tiles.

But the one thing I knew for certain was that a hospital visit wasn't the right move. I knew how that would play out. Back in the sixth grade, during Mack Dinwiddie's birthday party at the skate park, we were all acting stupid. Trying to pull off some tricks and impress the girls. Mack had just landed a frontside 180 on his new board, so of course I had to try. I popped just fine, but when I went for the spin, I lost my footing. I knew I'd broken my right arm as soon as I hit the concrete.

Mom had dropped me off at the party, so Mrs. Dinwiddie was the one who rushed me to the

ER. But the doctor wouldn't do a thing until Mom was called in and signed some paperwork.

So I knew. Five minutes with Clue's mom at the hospital and Mrs. Donoghue would figure it out.

"Why don't Clue and Nate stay over?" said Rodney, completely out of the blue. Clue and I cut our eyes at each other but didn't say a word. "Like you said, it's incredibly late, and we need to be well-rested for school tomorrow."

School.

Back in Shady Springs, we always got a week-long break after Thanksgiving. I'd assumed Clue and Rodney did too, but I guess not.

"Fine," said Mrs. Donoghue. "But I've at least got to call Katherine and let her know what's going on. She may still want you to see a doctor, dear." She nodded at Clue and began scrolling through her phone until she found the right contact. "Ah, there is she...."

Suddenly, Clue shifted her weight from off our shoulders and took a shaky step forward.

"Wait," she said weakly. She wrapped her arms around her ribcage, still wearing my coat I'd given her in the carriage. The oversized sleeves flopped past her fingertips. "Can I call?" said Clue. "I'd like to speak with her. I'll explain everything."

Mrs. Donoghue handed over the phone, and Clue pulled out her best acting chops.

She'd talk, pause, talk some more, pause, maybe nod. She even threw in a few *mhmm*'s and *sure thing*'s between chattering teeth. Clue carried on a very believable conversation. She had to. Mrs. Donoghue stood right there the entire time, no longer interested in her party, arms folded with one hand propped under her chin like she was *The Thinker*.

But Rodney and I both knew what was really going on. Mrs. Perez wasn't on the other end. There was no other cellphone.

It had been disconnected long ago.

CHAPTER 28

"Now," said Mrs. Donoghue, once Clue returned the phone, "let's get you into something dry and warm before you die of hypothermia."

She reached over, pressed an intercom button on the nearest wall, and called for a woman named Ingrid. In a matter of seconds, Ingrid — who was very stout and even shorter than Clue, which I didn't think was possible — scurried into the cavernous foyer wearing a black and white maid's uniform.

Ingrid nodded. "Mrs. Donoghue."

"Would you please escort Cluenette upstairs and run her a warm bath?" Mrs. Donoghue directed Clue into Ingrid's outstretched hands. "And let's see if we can get her some clothes that aren't sopping wet."

As Ingrid whisked Clue away, I followed Rodney to the kitchen, where a dozen chefs were cleaning pots and pans and mopping the floor. Things were wrapping up, but the fridges were packed with leftovers. I peeled back the plastic wrap and grabbed a couple of ham rolls while Rodney loaded a plate with olives, stuffed mushrooms, and some type of breaded chicken.

I scarfed down a roll in two bites.

Next time, I thought, *I'll eat* before *leaving Aunt Celeste's.*

We were sitting on bar stools along a giant stainless-steel island. The white coats had gone home for the night, but there was Rodney, still chowing down. I sat on my stool for a few more minutes, listening to him have at it, until I finally decided I couldn't take it any longer and went back for seconds. I grabbed a piece of that chicken and even treated myself to a chocolate mousse parfait.

"Hey, boys."

A surge of Christmas music filled the room as Mr. Donoghue entered the kitchen. He made a beeline for the silverware, found the biggest spoon he could, and immediately raided the freezer.

"I see you two had the same idea," he said, sitting down across from us with a tub of Neapolitan. He rolled up the sleeves of his red button-up and loosened his tie. It was freezing outside, but like my dad, the weather didn't seem to matter when it came to ice cream.

"Not enjoying the party?" said Rodney. He gave me a knowing grin.

"About as much as you are, I guess," said Mr. Donoghue, before downing a spoonful of strawberry. "Everyone seems to be leaving now, though. What a shame." He sighed and dug into the chocolate. "Just you two tonight?"

Rodney explained Clue's little mishap: Her fall. Her shakes. Her thawing out in the tub.

"That girl," said Mr. Donoghue, shaking his head. "She's something else. Remember when you two were little? She used to drag you all over the place on her crazy adventures."

I tried to picture mini-Clue and mini-Rodney running around the streets of New York together. Clue, the fearless leader, and Rodney, the faithful sidekick. Always going wherever Clue's wild imagination took them next.

"How did you guys meet?" I asked, suddenly curious.

Rodney finished his hundredth meatball and slid the plate away. "I guess you could say my mum sort of helped us become friends." Which wasn't hard to believe. Mrs. Donoghue did seem like the type who couldn't resist dipping her hands into everything. "It was soon after we'd arrived here from Australia," said Rodney. "She took me to some park, and it just so happened that Clue and Miss P were there too. Mum sat down on a bench while I ran over to the playground, and that's when I saw her. This girl surrounded by all the other kids. She had taken the broken plastic spaceship and somehow fastened it to the center of the merry-go-round."

Mr. Donoghue chuckled to himself, clearly a fan of the story.

"I walked up just as she was demonstrating her invention," Rodney continued. "She climbed in and got everyone to start counting down. Some of the kids began turning the merry-go-round, faster and faster. But I just watched. All I remember is wondering what would happen when they reached 'one'."

Rodney paused to take a drink.

"And?" I said. "What happened?"

"Clue took off like a *bullet*. She pulled some sort of lever, and I kid you not, that spaceship leaped straight off the platform and zoomed across the grass. Like she was actually flying. Everyone was cheering by that point, of course, and when the spaceship finally stopped, they all ran over to ask for a turn."

I shook my head and smiled. Of course that's how Clue spent her childhood. If someone were to ever write her biography, they'd connect the dots and somehow make a correlation between rigging playground equipment as an eight-year-old and future illegal activities that involved blowtorches, pulley systems, and tree charts.

"What about you? Did you take it for a spin?"

Rodney scratched his head and sort of laugh. "I just stood there. I think I was so impressed that that's all I *could* do. Even after the other kids left, I was still standing there like a statue. That's when she saw me." Rodney smiled, remembering. "She marched right over, shook my hand, and introduced herself like she'd been in business for twenty years. We started talking, she said she liked my accent, and the next thing I knew, we'd been playing for over an hour."

I clung to every word, enjoying this new peak into Clue's life. A glimpse into when things were simpler, brighter, and not so bleak. I wanted to hang on to those images. Of Clue racing around with a smile on her face. Of Mrs. Perez, energetic and fully present.

But that was only the prologue. From what I'd observed, Clue and her mom were now in the real meat of their story, just before the climax.

Those teetering few moments where you weren't sure how the book was going to end.

"Anyway," said Rodney, "once Mum met Mrs. Perez over by the swings, it was game over. She thought Clue went to Briars Academy too, so when she found out she went to public school in Brooklyn, she insisted on giving Clue a scholarship."

"Your mother was just trying to help," Mr. Donoghue offered with a smirk.

"That's one way of looking at it," said Rodney. "I personally like the theory that she was so desperate for me to have a friend, she'd have paid off a monkey."

Rodney later told me that Mrs. Donoghue always made "generous financial contributions" to Briars throughout the year, so she was able to pull a few strings with the board and get Clue in. (AKA she pumped the school with cash so, in return, she could run the place when it suited her.)

"Of course, Miss P. kept refusing," said Rodney while we were still huddled in the kitchen, "but as you can imagine, Mum usually doesn't take no for an answer."

Mr. Donoghue snapped the lid back on the ice cream carton, groaning as he stood. "Amen."

CHAPTER 29

Rodney loaned me a clean T-shirt and some sweats to sleep in. After brushing my teeth, I made my way back downstairs to the spacious living room where, for some random reason, we'd decided to crash for the night. I was sure the Donoghue's had plenty of spare bedrooms, but I think Rodney considered the situation to be more of a sleepover than the end of a very scary, very exhausting night.

Clue was already sprawled across the cream sofa when I walked in, wearing a robe and some sort of pink nightgown underneath. It was shocking to see her in anything besides overalls, but I bit my tongue to keep from saying so. Water still dampened her hair from the shower, and even from my pallet of pillows and blankets on the floor, I could smell the bodywash. It was nice, just different than her usual vanilla scent I'd come to…admire.

"What a night, yeah?" said Rodney as I sat down.

The coffee table had been pushed aside so the three of us could be in close proximity. Clue on the couch, Rodney and I spread out on the rug. A fire crackled in the marble fireplace, casting an orange glow around the room and everyone's faces.

"What a night," I agreed.

I wanted to ask Clue how she was feeling, but her eyes were closed. I didn't think she was asleep yet, but I got the impression she just wanted to lay in silence and not be bothered.

Silence.

A concept Rodney seriously struggled to understand.

"Tonight was *whack*; the bloke's not cuttin' us no *slack*," he started to rap. And then: "Oi! Anyone want some nachos? I know we just ate something, but I could really go for a pile of cheesy chili nachos. Or maybe we could gorge ourselves on a stack of greasy —"

"RODNEY."

Clue's voice cut straight through the gibberish. She didn't move from her position on the sofa, though. She just lay there among the tasseled pillows and silky cushions, staring up at the ornate ceiling.

"I'm wearing your mother's *underwear*," she hissed. "Which I'm pretty sure cost more than our monthly rent. I'm tired. I'm uncomfortable. I just nearly drowned, *and* we have school tomorrow."

Rodney thumbed toward the kitchen, still not comprehending. "Sooo…"

"So for the love of all that's good and holy, SHUT. UP."

There was a rare moment of silence where all you could hear was the faint honking of horns down below on Fifth Avenue, and then, out of nowhere, the meatballs started to betray him. Rodney released the longest, squeakiest fart. Like air slowly escaping a balloon.

I tried my best not to make a sound; I really did, for Clue's sake. We both held our breath for as long as possible, but it was no use. We started snickering uncontrollably —

Thump.

Two couch pillows pummeled our faces. After that, there was no more talk about late-night snacks. No more rapping. No more farting.

The only noise left was the crackling fire.

CHAPTER 30

I couldn't sleep. I tossed and turned for probably over an hour, but I guess I was too doped up on adrenaline. Climbing the Rockefeller Center Christmas Tree, putting out a fire, creeping through Central Park, saving Clue from an icy death — my mind was still racing from it all.

The electric logs continued burning, and outside, beyond the giant floor-to-ceiling windows, the city twinkled like some sort of metropolitan galaxy. It would've been a pretty serene setup had it not been for Rodney snoring like a chainsaw.

I sat up and pulled my knees to my chest. Clue looked peaceful as she slept on the couch. There were no pinched brows or frowning lips or rolling eyes. No disgusted sighs or signs of worry. She was breathing gently, finally getting the rest she deserved.

A lock of hair had strayed across Clue's face in her sleep. Quietly, I scooted across the rug until I was inches away from her. *She's so beautiful.* I finally let myself dwell on that thought because there was no point in denying it any longer. Clue was crazy and irrational and clever and protective and free-spirited and sometimes a little hotheaded.

And she was beautiful.

I slowly reached over and brushed the hair from her cheek, careful not to wake —

"What are you doing?"

I jerked my hand away and turned. Apparently Rodney had stopped snoring and was now sitting up watching me. He blinked lazily.

"Just can't sleep," I whispered, my heart throbbing. "Sorry."

The next few seconds seemed like hours. *Had he seen me? Did he think something was going on? Will he tell Clue? Am I freaking out for no reason?*

Nails dug into the palm of my hand as I clenched my fists, just waiting for him to respond. Waiting for him to grill me.

But he never did. Finally, Rodney shrugged and curled back under his blankets.

I killed some time by scrolling through my phone. Rodney's photography on his Instagram page was as mind-blowing as ever, and then I found myself in the family group chat. Mom had cleverly, in her eyes, named the group THE WILD(ER) FAMILY, which was ridiculous because we were the most boring bunch of suburbanites you could ever meet. My parents were addicted to routine and schedules. For instance, we rented the same house at the same beach during the same week every summer. We even stuck to the same dinner menu.

"Spontaneity" wasn't in the Wilder household's vocabulary.

Anyway, I started rereading some of the text messages, but the more I scrolled, the more I regretted it. Every conversation was the same. Reminders of how practical my life could be. There were links to our community college's business program..."You can help me cater this weekend!" offers from Mom...Dad's occasional hints about interning at his accounting firm.

Before I got too annoyed, I clicked out of there and opened the Notes app. I didn't want to think about business school, or catering, or filing random people's taxes.

I just wanted to write.

And since my notebook was MIA along with the backpack and spikes, my phone was my only option. So, I leaned against the couch — with Clue dreaming right by my shoulder — and started typing....

A girl is flying in her little orange spaceship. She's bound to have a name, but for now, it's only her mission that matters. She's flying, soaring, careening among the stars, looking this way and that.

"What are you looking for?" squeaks one tiny silver star.

"My mother," says the girl, and her spaceship zips on.

The girl's long hair waves behind her like a banner as she travels from one constellation to the next. She circles the Little Dipper, but her mother isn't there. She jets past the dragon's tail and the lion's mane, but her mother isn't among those stars either.

"I've lost her," the girl admits. "I've lost my mother."

Reluctantly, she turns, steering her spaceship back toward Earth. It's getting late.

"Wait," says a familiar voice. "Wait."

A warmth fills the girl's chest. *Could it be?* She slows her spaceship until it's almost hovering in place and peeks around the most beautiful golden star.

"Hello?" says the girl. "Who's there?"

And then the impossible happens. The star, as if it were a glowing globe, spins around to reveal its true face.

"Mother," says the girl, tears filling her eyes. "I thought you left. I thought you forgot about me."

The star smiles with a mother's gentleness, and the same familiar voice emerges: "You're my special girl," says the star. "Distance and time and even memory can never separate us. You'll remember that, won't you? Remember that I'll always be with you."

The girl nods, and even as she drifts back down to Earth, alone in her orange spaceship, she whispers the promise to herself. "I'll always be with you."

I'll always be with you.

CHAPTER 31

Clue was nowhere to be found the next morning. She'd disappeared. In fact, looking at the folded blanket and the couch's perfectly placed pillows, it was as if she was never there. Like she was some kind of phantom. Or Spiderman — Spider*woman*? — slinking through the city undetected.

"She certainly got an early start," mumbled Rodney, sitting up and rubbing his eyes.

I made a point not to look at him as I stacked my own blankets into a neat pile.

Does he remember last night? Is he about to ask a bajillion questions? Is he giving me that "I-saw-the-way-you-were-looking-at-her" look?

I didn't plan on finding out, so I kept my eyes glued to the task at hand.

"I reckon she's off to fix some brekkie for her mum before her morning shift."

Phew. No interrogation. Which meant he didn't remember. Or he just didn't care, which I would've also considered a win.

It was barely 6 a.m., but workers were already arriving to put the place back together after last night's party. Vacuums droned over the carpets, sponges scrubbed each tile, and feather dusters attacked every object in sight. Ingrid offered to have the kitchen prepare something special for Rodney and me, but we settled on bowls of Cinnamon Toast Crunch.

"If you see Mum," garbled Rodney, his mouth full, "*hide*." He wiped milk from his chin. "The most exciting cereal she lets us eat is Figs 'n' Fiber. Luckily, Ingrid always buys a box or two of the good stuff."

Looking at Rodney's hair, you'd have thought he'd stuck his hand in an electrical socket. It hadn't seen a comb yet, so the blonde mane was bushier than ever, curls spiraling out of control. Honestly, it almost gave Aunt Celeste's 'do a run for her money.

"Good to know," I said, munching away. When I finished, I leaned back and drained the last of the sugary milk from my bowl. Then I asked the question I knew was burning in everyone's mind: "Any ideas on where to start searching for this backpack?"

Rodney shook his head slowly, still at a loss. "You've got me, mate. I reckon Clue was on to something. Tracking down that bag will be like finding a box of sweets in a roo's pouch."

Of course it would. I almost felt stupid for thinking any differently, for having even the tiniest speck of hope. Finding one backpack in a city of eight million people was the definition of a needle in a haystack — or whatever craziness Rodney had said.

I had one job, same as everyone else, and I'd completely screwed it up. Clue was right. *It was over.* Defeated, I stood to carry my bowl to the kitchen.

"No way…."

Rodney rarely went anywhere without his camera, even in his own home. He'd dragged it over and was scrolling through photos, but something made him stop.

"What is it?"

"I took this on the train last night," he said. I set my bowl down so I could grab the camera he was shoving in my face. "Look at the bags!"

I couldn't believe what I was seeing. Next to my feet was the black backpack, but inches away, next to a pair of probably size 100 Nikes, was *another* backpack, almost identical.

And it belonged to the Hulk, my giant seat buddy in the gray sweats.

"He got off the train before us, right?" said Rodney. "What if he really did grab the wrong bag? He must've!"

I handed back the camera. "Too bad we don't know who he is. Maybe then we'd have a chance."

Rodney pulled the camera to his eye like he was checking out bacteria under a microscope. He kept zooming in on the photo until — "Wait a minute. Take a look at his shirt."

The stranger's gray hoodie was unzipped just enough to see a colorful T-shirt logo stretched

across his chest. "The...Lucky Duck Laundromat."
I shook my head and shrugged. "So?"

Without saying another word, Rodney ran from the dining room.

"Where are you going?" I called, but the only answer was his feet stomping up the stairs.

A minute later, Rodney returned out of breath. *"Look,"* he panted, pressing a gold coin into my hand.

It was about the size of a quarter, but instead of ole George W., it was engraved with the image of a cartoon duck playing a pinball machine. The same image on mystery-dude's T-shirt.

"The Lucky Duck," I said, turning the coin over, weighing it in my hand. "Is this what they make you pay with to wash your dirty socks?"

Rodney plucked it from my palm. "No," he said, "you don't get it. This is a token for the arcade hidden *inside* the laundromat."

"The what?"

"It's pretty elite, actually," said Rodney proudly. "Most people don't know about it. Plus," he added, "you can't get in without one of these." He twirled the coin between his fingers like a piece of treasure.

"So you've been to this arcade?" I asked. "How did *you* find out about it?"

"Conner…Something-or-other had a birthday party there in fifth grade. Everybody in our class got a bag of these to take with them, but I held on to one because I thought they were cool. Good thing, too!"

Just then, the intercom crackled, and Mrs. Donoghue's polished voice filled the room. "Rodney," she said, "the car will be here in fifteen minutes if you want a ride to school. Fifteen minutes."

Rodney nodded. "Right. Well, I'll stop by The Lucky Duck after school and hopefully get this mess all sorted. Maybe the bag is even —"

"No way," I cut in. "Let me do it. Please. If not, I'll be stuck inside feeding Gerdy Cool Ranch Doritos all day."

Aunt Celeste's big *Wicked* debut was this week, so her rehearsal schedule had been pretty grueling. She'd be gone for at least the next twelve hours. Taking on "Operation Lucky Duck" would free me from goat-sitting — *and* give me a chance to prove I was somewhat less of an idiot.

I grabbed Rodney's camera and used my phone to take a picture of the guy in gray. With any luck, someone at the arcade would recognize him and at least point me in the right direction.

"Okay," said Rodney after a moment's pause, "but only if you're sure." He made to drop the coin in my hand but stopped short. "This is my only one," he said, eyebrows raised. "Once you use it to get in, that's it; we can't go back there."

He finally surrendered the coin.

"So make your visit count, mate."

CHAPTER 32

I had texted Aunt Celeste late last night after Rodney announced we were sleeping over, but she'd probably been snoozing for hours on the couch by then, so she didn't respond until the next morning when Rodney and I were scarfing down Cinnamon Toast Crunch.

OK B SAFE OUT THERE IM HEADING TO REHEARSAL EGG SALAD IN FRIDGE IF YOU WANT SOME

That was the difference between Mom and Aunt Celeste. If I was out with friends a second past 9 p.m., you could bet Mom would be pacing the floor with phone in hand, ready to speed dial the FBI and start a whole search and rescue. But Aunt Celeste? She'd apparently go into a popcorn coma until dawn without ever realizing I was gone.

I replied to her text with a simple thumbs up.

Mrs. Donoghue insisted on her car service driving me to wherever I needed to go. I was planning on taking a taxi, but she practically dragged me into the spotless, gleaming SUV that awaited us outside. "Don't be silly," she said, sliding on a long cashmere coat. "That's what the service is for, dear. Pierre doesn't mind."

Rodney climbed in the back while Mrs. Donoghue and I took the two middle seats. If Pierre minded, he sure didn't show it. His face was about as expressive as one of those bearskin-hat guards at Buckingham Palace.

The car cruised effortlessly down Fifth Avenue, and as corny as it sounds, I got the warmest feeling that we were driving through a winter wonderland. Every Christmas light and decoration sparkled under the overcast sky. Good thing, too. As Mrs. Donoghue blabbed away on her phone, going over some marketing budget nonsense for the magazine, it was nice to have some sort of distraction from all her yapping.

I couldn't pull my eyes away from the magic of it all. Wintery scenes filled the storefront windows, each one like a colorful snow globe surrounded by brick and mortar. Every moment that passed offered something new to look at — a giant toy chest, a larger-than-life teddy bear, a glowing hot air balloon, and so many other installations along the busy street.

After catching a glimpse of Cartier, which was lit up to perfectly resemble a gold present wrapped in red ribbon, we made a few turns and eventually arrived at a large stone building full of history and architecture. *Briars Academy.* Pierre pulled the car over and hopped out to open the door for Rodney.

Before Rodney headed inside, though, he turned and pressed a fist to his chest. He nodded. Wishing me luck.

The Lucky Duck Laundromat wasn't much to look at. In fact, if you *weren't* looking for it, you'd probably miss the whole thing altogether. It was a little square of cement wedged between a pharmacy and some Chinese restaurant that had closed ages ago. Faded advertisements crowded the front window so you couldn't even see inside.

"Diane, could you hold, please?"

Mrs. Donoghue finally stopped talking and muted her phone. She leaned forward so she could see around me, getting a good look at the laundromat.

"Blimey," she whispered slowly. "You sure this is where you need to go?" She gave it one more glance over before shaking her head. "Bit of a dog's breakfast, don't you think?"

"I'm sure," I said, just as Pierre opened my door. I stood on the sidewalk, right next to what had to be the world's biggest pile of garbage, and thanked Mrs. Donoghue again for the lift.

The SUV sped away, leaving me alone with a backpack full of weapons and staring at a yellowed sign above the door that now read **UCKY DU LAUNDROMAT**.

For at least the next thirty seconds, I couldn't help but wonder if I'd made a terrible mistake.

CHAPTER 33

A tiny bell chimed as I walked in, but the customers paid me no mind.

The place was your regular run-of-the-mill laundromat. An ancient TV in the corner near the ceiling was collecting dust and playing some *I Love Lucy* rerun. People shuffled around with all the joy of a dead cockroach — quietly matching socks, folding pants, pushing carts, dumping bed sheets into the wash…you get the idea.

The space was much longer than I expected. Stacked washing machines lined both sides of the laundromat, their large, metal frames built into the walls. As I walked through, I passed load after load of soapy clothes spinning behind circular glass doors.

My hand squeezed around the gold coin in my coat pocket. *What do I do with this?* I thought. Rodney had said the arcade was inside the laundromat…but that was it. No further explanation. And from what I could tell, there was no pinball or air hockey in sight.

Only baskets full of hideous underwear.

I kept walking and discovered the laundromat wasn't just a long rectangle after all. It curved to the right, forming a giant L shape. I rounded the corner and found even more washing machines, but no one was using them, I assumed, because it was much darker back here. Half of the fluorescent lights were either blown or missing completely. One of them flickered overhead like some haunted hallway I'd seen in a movie once.

If I was Peter Parker, I'd have said my spidey sense was tingling. Not because of any impending danger, but because I had a strange feeling that I was in the right place. That I was where I was supposed to be — without the whole Green Goblin thing.

I pulled out the Lucky Duck coin and walked deeper into the shadows; the whir and rattle of machines in use around the corner seemed a million miles away now. Clue and Rodney were well into class, but I considered unclipping the walkie-talkie from my waistband and radioing in anyway. Because even though I felt like I was close, I still didn't really know what I was looking for.

But, instead of worrying myself into a spiral, I did what Rodney would do.

I started singing.

"Oh, where, oh, where has my lucky duck gone?" I began mumbling, tweaking the song I still remembered from kindergarten. "Oh, where, oh, where can he be?" Everything seemed a bit too dark and fuzzy — and not just because of the lack of overhead lighting. I took off my glasses and realized they were covered in a layer of lint dust, so I blew it off and slid my glasses back up my nose. I blinked, trying to readjust my vision. "Oh, where, oh, where has my lucky duck gone? Oh, where, oh, where can he —"

That's when I saw it.

My eyes landed on the top washing machine in front of me. The dingy lights weren't hitting on much, but still, I knew what I was looking at.

Engraved very faintly on the circular glass door — just that one door — was the image of a duck playing pinball.

"This is it," I breathed excitedly, stealing a glance around the corner to make sure nobody was paying attention.

This is it.

And suddenly it all made sense. Suddenly I knew what I was supposed to do. I stepped up to the machine, coin in hand, and pushed it into the coin slot. It clinked and clanked as it dropped through a series of hidden mechanisms, before ending with a solid *plunk*.

The coin stopped...but nothing else happened.

No smoke. No strobe lights. No congratulatory theme song to let me know it had worked.

What if it didn't? I thought miserably. *What if I've wasted the coin — our only coin — and it didn't even work?*

I waited a few more seconds, hoping for a miracle, but nothing changed.

My stomach sank as my entire body slumped forward. I rested an arm against the wall of washing machines to prop myself up. There was a burn behind my eyes, a mix of anger and disappointment.

Way to go, Nate. WAY TO GO.

All I wanted was to prove myself to Clue. That I could retrieve the backpack and make things right. But she would just be disappointed all over again. And once I told Rodney, he'd wish he'd handled this himself like he originally wanted.

"Uh, sir, you okay?"

The voice broke through my anxious thoughts and opened my eyes. I peeled myself away from the wall, and when I turned, a pudgy, forty-something-year-old woman was standing just a few feet away, hands on her hips. The nametag pinned to her navy Lucky Duck polo read DENISE.

"Can I help you with somethin'?"

I blinked out the sting in my eyes and took a few more steps back. "I just…" I awkwardly pointed at the washing machine, the one with the Lucky Duck logo. "I was…"

"You needin' to get into the arcade?" said Denise. She shook her head and casually flicked her wrist. "This thing is so old. Been eatin' people's coins up for *months*. Sometimes you just gotta give it a lil extra lovin'."

With that, Denise sacrificed her whole body by ramming her shoulder into the stack of washing machines. I sort of jumped back, surprised, and quickly glanced around, wondering if anyone else noticed. Then Denise beat her fist twice over the circular glass door — *boom boom* — before finishing with a single knuckle rap right above the coin slot.

CLICK.

The moment I heard it, I knew she'd succeeded; her trick had worked. Denise brushed her hands together like her secret-door-opening-skills were simply "all in a day's work," nodded, and then disappeared around the corner again.

"Enjoy!" she called back, just as the door began to moan under shifting weight.

And by *door*, I mean the exterior of the two washing machines in front of me. As it turned out, they weren't washers at all. Their stacked doors were connected, forming one giant rectangle with two circular windows, sort of like a silver domino.

The door creaked open, but all it revealed was a dark hallway. Still no pinball or air hockey anywhere. I took a deep breath, held it for a moment, and then slowly released, stretching out the seconds for as long as possible.

Here goes nothing, I thought.

Before stepping into complete, utter darkness.

CHAPTER 34

Every step felt like I was walking toward my death.

The farther I went, the more I realized I'd gladly climb a hundred Rockefeller Center Christmas Trees — wind, flimsy branches, and all — if it meant I didn't have to trek through another dark tunnel like this one. It felt like the beginning of some bad murder mystery. Or that part in a horror film when you start yelling at the screen, begging the protagonist not to go inside the creepy house.

My mind exploded with a million questions. *Does this actually lead to an arcade?* being the main one.

It seemed more likely I would stumble onto a drug deal.

If I was abducted or beaten to death, I'd never be found. My parents would spend the rest of their lives wondering what happened to me, and here I'd be, corpse rotting, my bones decaying beneath a New York City laundromat. A pile of dust for the rats to play in.

Thump thump.

Blood pounded in my ears as my heart began to race.

Thump. Thump THUMP.

My heart. Now it was going crazy.

Thump THUMP thump THUMP thump THUMP THUMP.

Hold up. Since when did my heartbeat sound like…One Direction?

The farther I walked, the brighter the tunnel became. Darkness morphed into a hazy gray, and music was definitely playing somewhere in the distance. It wasn't my heart at all. I kept walking, and before I knew it, the hall opened into a gloomy room filled with every kind of arcade game you could imagine, the air glowing with blue, pink, and green neon lights.

So there is *an arcade.*

Relief rushed through me as I weaved through a maze of games — Whac-A-Mole, Pac-Man, Fruit Ninja, and yes, even a couple of pinball machines. Some little girl with pigtails was on her tiptoes, clobbering plastic moles with a rubber mallet while her mom cheered her on.

I hurried past them and finally found the ticket counter. A couple of workers — probably college students — stood behind a glass counter filled with cheap prizes.

"Can I help you?" asked the girl chewing a wad of gum. She leaned over the counter and continued scrolling through her phone, somehow sensing my presence.

"Uhh…I hope so," I said, digging my own phone from my pocket. I found the photo and slid it under her nose. "You don't know him, do you? He's wearing a Lucky Duck shirt, so I thought someone around here might —"

"Yeah, I know him." The girl sucked in a deep breath as she stood up straight and cracked her back. She turned and called for someone named Thad, but her voice was interrupted by a dramatic yawn. When she'd finished yawning, and when no one responded, she finally worked up a little more energy. *"Thad!"*

She shook her head and hunched over her phone again, resuming her scrolls. Thankfully, Thad must've heard her, because some guy emerged from the back room, his broad shoulders barely squeezing through the doorframe.

It was definitely him. The same giant from the subway.

The same guy who had our spikes.

But that also meant...he was the same one missing a bag full of *weapons*. I swallowed hard, suddenly wondering — all over again — if I'd made a big mistake coming here. But it didn't matter. It was too late to make a run for it. The girl nodded toward me, and Thad stepped around the counter, running a tattooed hand over his buzzcut.

"You need something?" he said, his voice deep and sort of annoyed.

Thad was a *beast* — more so than I remembered. He was like a twenty-year-old John Cena. Even his gleaming forehead had muscles.

"Hey, Thad." I stood as tall as possible, hoping to give myself at least a couple more centimeters.

"It's Thaddeus," he boomed. "Only my friends call me Thad."

Gulp.

"Right," I said, nodding and swallowing way too much. It suddenly felt like a fist was wrapped around my throat. "Anyway, I know you're probably super busy and stuff, but my friends and I...we...think, maybe, we switched backpacks with you. Last night. On the subway."

The scowl on Thaddeus' face lifted for just a second, and I knew he knew what I was talking about. He crossed his arms over his massive chest.

"So *you're* the little thief who took my bag."

I didn't know which was more humiliating — being called *little* or a *thief.*

"Well, actually," I said, "I think you got off the train first."

Thaddeus dropped his tree-trunk arms and closed the gap between us. "You calling *me* a thief?"

Yep. I definitely should've let Rodney handle this one.

"Of course not," I said. "I just think…maybe there was a little mix-up. The bags are almost identical, so maybe —"

"I'm just messing with you, dude," said Thaddeus. His fist bump to my arm nearly knocked me over. "It's a good thing you showed up. I thought I was going to have to cancel today if I didn't get my stuff back."

Cancel what? I thought. *Your next murder?*

"Is that it?" said Thaddeus, reaching for the backpack slung over my shoulder.

I took a step back. "Yeah…but I'm hoping we can trade now." *Gulp.* Every word that spilled from my mouth felt like another dig in an already-deep hole. Another nail in the coffin. "Do you have my bag with you?"

"Nah. It's over at the boxing gym, in my locker, I think." Thaddeus nodded over his shoulder. "I'm headed there now if you want to come."

A boxing gym? That was a twist. I expected to run into the arcade, exchange backpacks, and be out in under ten. What if the boxing gym was just an excuse? What if there *was* no gym? What if this Thaddeus guy planned on beating me to a pulp in some dark alley and then chopping me up with his bag full of weapons?

What if I was a *60 Minutes* special in the making?

I don't have a choice, I determined. *Either trust him…or walk away empty-handed.*

CHAPTER 35

Thaddeus said the gym was only a few blocks away, so we just walked. He led the way — a boulder of pure muscle plodding down the sidewalk — and I sort of trailed behind. I wanted to keep my distance in case I needed to make a run for it.

Thaddeus could crush me with his pinky, but I figured I might at least be faster.

I'd read enough thrillers to know you don't look away in these kinds of situations. You stay focused and alert, because the moment you let your guard down...well, just use your imagination. So I kept my head up; I didn't even pull out my phone to see where we were. It was definitely a less glamorous side of Manhattan, that's for sure. The buildings were older, shorter, and the Christmas decorations weren't nearly as nice.

Mom was always particular about the kind of garland she hung around the house. She made sure it actually *looked* like real pinecones, needles, and berries, as opposed to the cheap plastic stuff.

Needless to say, Mom wouldn't use the garland around this neighborhood. The Christmas lights either. They decorated many of the graffitied doorways and arches and columns, but it was impossible to find a strand that wasn't half blown or didn't look like a two-year-old had strung it up.

No wonder Mrs. Donoghue got out of here so quickly, I thought.

She probably got hives just being around such tacky décor.

We turned down another side street, and I was relieved to see there was an actual gym, because it made me feel a little bit better about my chances of survival. Maybe Thaddeus wouldn't slit my throat after all. Maybe he was telling the truth.

The gym was nothing special really, just an old warehouse with a blue boxing ring planted in the middle of the concrete floor. Vintage light fixtures hung from the rafters, each one enclosed in a metal cage.

Feels like a Rocky *movie*, I thought.

But then I saw the cosplayers — people dressed up as all kinds of ninjas and warriors — and it suddenly felt like New York Comic Con.

"What is this?" I asked as Thaddeus and I approached a group huddled near the ring.

He spread out his massive arms and gestured to the crowd. "Welcome," he said proudly, "to the Mortal Kombat League of the Lower East Side." People nodded, some waved, and a few even struck a fighting pose before aggressively shouting, "Finish him!"

"Mortal Kombat..." I studied the strange, over-zealous group around me. "Like the old video game?"

"Exactly," said Thaddeus. And I could tell by the weird gleam in his eyes that Mortal Kombat meant as much to him as writing meant to me.

Twenty minutes later and I still didn't have my backpack. Thaddeus was too busy walking around, fist bumping, and slapping backs with the other players to remember. I followed behind him like a lost puppy, but every time I opened my mouth to ask for the bag, he was already chatting it up with someone new.

"Thad, you got the rest of the weapons, right?" some player threw out.

"Yeah," said Thaddeus. "Little dude's got 'em." He nodded in my direction, and all I could do was stand there with a stupid half-grin on my face, secretly grinding my teeth to the gums. The "little" jokes were getting old. If only he knew all the insane (not to mention *illegal*) stuff I'd done over the past two days, he'd think differently. But it wasn't just that.

I was also beating myself up over the fact that Rodney, Clue, and I had apparently been freaking out over fake cosplay weapons.

"Thaddeus —" I started for the millionth time. But he was already midsentence with some warrior in a pointed gold hat named Scott.

"Is Demetri not coming? He's usually here by now."

Scott double-checked a text before answering. "Doesn't look like it," he sighed. "Said he thinks he's got food poisoning."

This must've been devastating news, because suddenly everyone within earshot was in on the conversation. It seemed serious — plus I couldn't have cared less — so I stepped outside the huddle and let them have at it.

Finally, Scott removed his hat and shrugged. "Guess your team will have to forfeit."

"No way," Thaddeus boomed.

"Then what do you propose we do?"

Thaddeus took a while to respond, huffing and puffing enough to blow an entire village of little pigs' houses down. He shook his head and stared up at the ceiling.

"You're down a team member," said Scott. "You don't really have a choice."

But then, since he stood about a foot taller than everyone else, I watched as Thaddeus slowly turned in my direction. And I knew exactly what he was thinking. I could see it written in his eyes.

"No way," I said, my thumbs still tucked under the straps of Thaddeus' backpack.

Over my dead body.

CHAPTER 36

Long story short, I ended up joining the Mortal Kombat League of the Lower East Side. Just for one afternoon.

This Demetri dude was apparently supposed to play Sub-Zero, some ice ninja. I don't know. But since he was at home puking his guts out from a platter of bad sushi, I had the special honor of wearing his costume. After some debate with Thaddeus in a quiet corner of the gym, I agreed to help his team if he promised to exchange bags the moment the competition was over.

We shook on it, which was its own kind of torture. Thaddeus' grip was like a metal vise. If he hadn't have let go when he did, I'm pretty sure my fingers would've popped right off.

Demetri must've been about fifty pounds heavier than me and quite a bit taller, because the blue ninja mantel hung off my shoulders like a trash bag, and the pants were about five inches too long. Thaddeus pulled the small axe from his backpack

I'd been lugging around all morning and shoved it in my hand.

"Here's your ice scepter," he said quickly. "No head shots and nothing below the belt. Arms and stomach are ten points, and chest is thirty. Got it?"

I pushed back the black hood that was slipping over my eyes. "Uhhh…"

Before I could ask any questions, Thaddeus was already rushing toward the ring for Round One.

The announcer sat at a flimsy card table, and as he spoke into one of those portable karaoke machines, his voice squealed around the gym. We all ducked away, clamping our hands over our ears.

"Sorry," he mumbled into the microphone. And then, once the feedback faded, he began waving a tiny green flag.

"FIIIIIGHT!"

Thaddeus and his opponent immediately jumped into action. They slowly circled the ring, half crouched in some weird praying mantis-stance, sizing each other up. From what I'd gathered, Thaddeus was playing the character of Smoke — half ninja, half cyborg. His costume consisted of a bunch of black armored plates, which was probably supposed to look intimidating.

To me, he just looked like a big black beetle.

They began growling at each other, and eventually, the weapons came out. Thaddeus retrieved a couple of knives from his belt while his lizard-like rival did the same. Their knives swatted through the air, cutting and slicing all over the place. Thaddeus' team cheered when he landed a stab in Reptile's stomach.

"Ten points for Smoke!" shouted the announcer.

CHAPTER 37

To no one's surprise, Thaddeus won his match by a landslide.

And then it was on to the next match. Then the next. I paced back and forth and took more than one leisurely stroll around the gym's perimeter as players fought each other two at a time. Axes flung, swords pierced, and whips snapped over and over again. Unfortunately, every time an announcement was made, a penalty was called, points were given, or a match began or ended, the announcer felt the need to beat his tiny tabletop gong. He beat it so much that I thought for sure I'd be hearing that annoying *bonggg!* in my sleep for the rest of my life.

Hours later, I heard the words I'd been dreading since I first pulled on my costume.

"Sub-Zero. Goro. You're up!"

Suddenly, all of the room's energy evaporated. Every creature, ninja, and warrior froze. People gasped.

As I made my way to the ring, I passed by the announcer's card table. "What's wrong?" I whispered.

But he'd grown quiet too. All he could do was stare at me with a look of deep concern, cross himself, and mutter some sort of prayer.

As I approached the ring, I could feel every eye in the room on my skin, despite the oversized hood. However, the moment I ducked under the ropes and crawled onto the mat, I knew what all the fuss was about.

I was facing Goro — a fighter even bigger than Thaddeus.

I hadn't seen him all day, probably because he'd been off doing a thousand pushups or gargling nails. Seriously, the guy was Jason Momoa-massive. The only stitch of clothing he wore was some sort of leather loincloth and two leather wristbands. His muscles were the only armor he needed.

My eyes scanned the crowd pressing in around the ring, and all I could think about were those gladiator fights we'd discussed in history class once. The brutal matches where people watched one fighter murder the other in a sandy pit. *For fun.*

I eventually found Thaddeus standing just outside the ropes. He shrugged and wore the kind of worried expression you'd expect from a family member waving their youngest off to war.

It was nice knowing you, his face seemed to say. *Rest in peace, little dude.*

Then that stupid gong sounded — and it was on.

Goro stomped toward me like an oversized mountain troll. But what was *I* supposed to do? I just stood there like an idiot. Part of me felt ridiculous, dressed up in some baggy costume with a bunch of twenty-year-olds clutching toy weapons. The other part of me was terrified.

Thankfully, instincts kicked in just as Goro reached for me, and I jumped out of the way. I ran to the other side of the mat, but Goro was on my heels in seconds.

OOF!

Before I even had time to think of where to run next, Goro's fist smashed against my ribs. I doubled over as all the air rushed out of me. I gulped and gasped and tried my best to refill my lungs. Still, the pain was nothing compared to what it would've been without the protective padding under my costume.

Somehow, I shakily pulled myself upright again. But it was no use. Goro hoisted his weight high into the air and spun around like Jackie Chan. As he did, he stretched out one of his legs just long enough for his foot to collide with my face.

My jaw cracked, and my entire body toppled sideways. Loud *Ooohhh*'s rippled around the ring.

I'm dying here, I thought, crouched on my knees and fumbling for my glasses. They'd flung off somewhere across the slippery mat. *This is it. This is how I'm going.*

Which was all pretty ironic. The closest I'd ever come to a fight was second grade gym class.

Chad Masoncup lied and told everyone *he* won the baton race. So I pushed him and he fell. The end.

Fast forward and I was now being beaten to death by Goliath in what had to be the sketchiest part of Manhattan.

"Sub-Zero! Get up!"

I groaned and tried to blink away the blur. There, just a few feet away, peering through the ropes, was Thaddeus.

"Get up!" he shouted again.

His arm reached onto the mat, where my glasses had apparently sailed, and slid them my way. "You can do this," he said. *"You're faster than he is."*

Maybe. Maybe not. Honestly, I was hurting too much to think about it.

But one thing was certain: I'd never get those spikes back by lying around on this greasy mat.

Clue and Rodney needed me. We were a team now. I'd lost the spikes, and so it was up to me to get us back on track.

I wiped the sweat from my eyes and popped my glasses back on. My cheek was still on fire from Goro's spin kick, but it would just have to burn. All that mattered in that moment was getting up and giving this fight my best shot. For Clue. For Rodney. *For me.* I planted my fists into the mat and pushed off. When I stood, Goro was towering over me, ready to deliver another blow.

But I dodged it.

His fist swung right, so I pivoted the same. I raced to the other side of the mat, and when he turned, we were back to where we had started. Staring at each other.

Still heaving, I took a brave step forward and swung my ice scepter wildly through the air. I felt like a fool. The weapon was clumsy in my hands, so I wasn't surprised when it landed nowhere near Goro. He chuckled as we slowly circled one another.

Then, as we continued moving, he reached behind his back to retrieve something. I couldn't tell

what it was. He squeezed the thing with his fist —
and then unleashed it.

Whatever it was came flying at me like a
fastball. By some miracle, I sidestepped it just in
time. It landed like putty on the mat next to me,
some sort of green blob. A wad of snot? Or the
flubber stuff from that Robin Williams' movie.

"Watch out for his green fireballs!"
Thaddeus shouted.

*Green fireballs. You've got to be kidding
me....*

Just when I thought this whole thing
couldn't get any crazier.

I didn't know where Goro kept the fireballs
stashed — some secret compartment in his
loincloth? — but he kept whipping them out like
candy.

"Offense!" said Thaddeus.

Which is hard to do when you're constantly
bouncing from side to side, dodging snot rockets.

But he was right. The bunny hop was getting
me nowhere, so when Goro reached for his next

fireball, I took off. I ran straight toward him, full speed, and just as I reached his thunder thighs, I dropped and slid right through. Blood pounded in my ears, but I'm pretty sure I heard some gasps from the audience too.

I came out on the other side, and before Goro could turn, I jumped to my feet. With a firm grip, I brought the ice scepter down.

Straight into the middle of Goro's back.

CHAPTER 38

Thaddeus' team — *our* team — sounded off like a football stadium. They clapped and yelled and jumped up and down as soon as the announcement was made. According to the Mortal Kombat League of the Lower East Side's handbook (Yes, it's a thing. And yes, I was just as surprised.), my ice scepter move was considered a death blow. A kind of sudden death, even if it was one hundred percent pure luck. Which meant...

I won.

I actually won the final match.

Goro clapped me on the back with the force of an elephant, and then Thaddeus rushed onto the platform with a goofy smile.

"You really stuck it to him, little dude," he said, beaming like a proud older brother. "I *knew* you could do it."

Somehow the 'little dude' thing didn't seem so negative anymore.

"NATE!"

I looked around Thaddeus just in time to see Rodney climbing through the ropes. He pried them apart as wide as he could, but one of his feet still caught on a rubbery cord as he stepped through, throwing him to the mat.

"I'm alright!" He jumped back up without missing a beat. "I'm alright." Rodney paused long enough to snap a photo of me in my costume and then ran over. "That was *brilliant*, mate! I didn't know you could do kung fu!"

Thaddeus looked as if he wanted to say something, but he let it go.

"Thanks," I said, finally able to start undoing every button, sash, and zipper that held me captive. "How did you find me?"

"Well, I didn't hear an update on" — Rodney paused, noticing the curious eyes and ears all around — "*things*...so I caught a cab to the Lucky Duck after school. Reckoned I'd better make sure you weren't dead in a ditch or something. Girls there said you'd taken off for the boxing ring, so they were kind enough to give me the address. And boy am I glad they did. Otherwise I'd have missed seeing my pal Nate Wilder absolutely *crushing* it!" He shook my shoulders excitedly. "Wait 'til Clue hears about this one."

"Hang on. How did you make it into the arcade? I thought you gave me the last coin."

Rodney tugged his beanie down to his yellow eyebrows. "I...may have held on to one," he said with a toothy, sheepish grin. "Just in case."

After a brief announcement about next week's tournament, everyone said goodbye and went their separate ways. Most members didn't bother changing out of their costumes, which I thought was weird. But I guess a ninja or lizard-man walking down the street wasn't the strangest thing to see in New York.

Rodney stuck around while Thaddeus and I traded backpacks. It was stashed in his gym locker, just like he'd said, and when he passed the bag over, everything in the world immediately felt right again, the spikes' familiar weight on my back strangely comforting.

"Thanks, Thaddeus. We really appreciate this."

"It's Thad," he said, offering me a fist bump. "And I should be thanking *you*. You really saved our skins out there today. Tell you what," he said as he dug in his pocket, "here's my card. You need anything, just let me know."

"Wow. Thanks."

Thad shrugged. "Of course. You're an honorary League member now. Consider yourself one of us."

That was the last thing I wanted, but I studied the card anyway, out of respect. As far as business cards go, this one wasn't much. Just some cheesy WordArt on white cardstock.

THE MORTAL KOMBAT LEAGUE	
OF THE LOWER EAST SIDE	
Smoke	**Phone:** 212-555-0101
(Thaddeus Keppler)	**Email:** TheSmokeMachine@MKcosplay.net

I tucked the card inside my coat. "I'll remember that."

Rodney and I turned to leave, me with all my aching battle scars, but just as we were about to step outside —

"Hang on." Thad pointed to my backpack. "What are those things, anyway? They looked pretty expensive."

"Uhh…" I glanced nervously at Rodney, too exhausted to think on my feet. A hot shower was about the only thing running through my mind at the moment.

But Rodney just smiled and explained in the most calm, rational way: "Christmas decorations."

CHAPTER 39

Rodney and I caught the subway to Central Park so we could hide the two spikes along with the others. It was broad daylight, something we'd all sworn to avoid when stashing the goods, but time was a luxury we couldn't afford. We had more to steal that night and needed all hands on deck.

(Just thinking that way made my stomach turn.)

We were very careful, though. Stealth mode to the highest level. Rodney patrolled the perimeter of the Cop Cot rotunda, whistling while he kept an eye on things, and I quickly buried the spikes before anyone noticed.

In. Out. *Done.*

"Well, see ya tonight, mate," said Rodney once we exited the park.

He jogged across Fifth Avenue for what I'm sure was a Michelin-star-worthy dinner. As for me? I braved another smelly, crowded train back to Brooklyn.

Aunt Celeste's debut was only a few days away, so she wouldn't be home from practice until well after dark. I took the longest shower of my life, breathing in the steam and letting the hot water roll over every sore muscle. Afterward, I peeked inside the fridge at the egg salad Aunt Celeste had mentioned. Was it supposed to be that green?

I closed the door with a shudder.

Hard pass.

Unsurprisingly, I found Gerdy in the kitchen surrounded by her truckload of toys. "Want to go for a walk?" I asked. She immediately began bleating. "I'll take that as a yes."

Ralph's Mini-Mart was only ten minutes away. I knew I could get a decent cappuccino there because Aunt Celeste and I had stopped by yesterday before church, and nothing sounded better in that moment than something hot, foamy, and caffeinated. A cold mist had started to fall, so I snapped on Gerdy's bright yellow raincoat before leaving.

Because I knew Aunt Celeste. She'd want her "Gerdy Girl" to stay dry.

Ralph's customers paid the goat no mind — even though she looked like the Gorton's fisherman from one of those boxes of breaded fish sticks. I could only assume they'd seen much worse. After filling up a sixteen-ounce cup to the brim, I popped on a lid and headed for the front counter. But Gerdy wasn't feeling very patient. Before I could stop her, she yanked on the leash and nuzzled her nose into the back of the customer's knee in front of us. The girl turned around.

"Clue?"

I pulled Gerdy away from her legs. "I'm sorry about that. This thing is crazy."

"No worries."

Clue's apartment was just a few blocks from Aunt Celeste's, so it made sense she'd be hitting up the same sketchy convenience store.

"Gerdy needed some exercise, and I needed the caffeine. What about you?"

Clue held up the discounted loaf she'd been hugging in line. "Out of bread. Since Mom torched every slice in the apartment last night." She sighed before adding, "Plus, Miss Mable'll be coming over to watch her soon. I figured she may want a sandwich."

"That's nice of you."

Clue nodded, but her eyes were already pulled away, aimlessly roaming around the store. She didn't seem to be looking at anything. Not really. She just seemed...quiet. Distracted. No snarky comments about Gerdy's coat was one thing. But the purple bruise already puffing across my cheekbone? That was prime real estate for Clue jokes.

But she didn't say a word.

"You okay?"

Clue rocked back on her heels, and I could see the chords of tension as she bit the inside of her jaw. "Yeah," she said softly. "Just uh...just a little tired."

I could only imagine. A 5 a.m. shift at Java the Hut, school, and rushing home to fix dinner — all while trying to pull off some insane heist — would be a lot for anyone.

Not to mention topping it all off with a dunk in the icy Pond.

"Next!"

The cashier summoned Clue forward. As she waited to be rang up, one of her elbows disappeared from her side; her head tilted forward. And I couldn't help but wonder if she was crying.

After paying for my cappuccino, I hurried out the store and caught up with Clue in the parking lot, Gerdy's hooves clicking right behind me.

"Hey," I said, a little out of breath. "Can I take you somewhere?"

Clue stared at me then, her chocolate eyes thinning suspiciously. Gerdy sniffed at the bag of bread dangling by her knees.

I swallowed and quickly tried to steer the train back on track. "Sorry," I said. "I mean, can you meet me at the subway in, like, twenty minutes? The one on 36th." It didn't seem possible, but a thousand more concerns crossed Clue's face. I cleared my throat. "If you can."

Silence.

Nothing but the rumble of passing cars and someone shouting in the distance.

The longer we stood there in the cold, the redder Clue's nose turned — and the more obnoxious Gerdy became. Smelling was no longer enough. She started clacking her teeth together like some ventriloquist dummy, hoping for a nibble.

Finally, Clue nodded. "Sure."

I bit my tongue to keep from smiling too much. "Yeah? Okay, great!" I said, tugging on Gerdy's leash before she came away with a mouthful of bread. "See you then."

CHAPTER 40

I almost didn't think she was coming.

I sat next to the subway entrance for a good ten minutes, watching every kind of runner, dogwalker, mail carrier, Uber driver, and pizza delivery boy pass by — everybody *except* Clue. But then she rounded the corner in those familiar black overalls and boots, and I felt bad for ever doubting she'd show.

I met her at the top of the stairs, and we trudged down them together. "How's your mom?" I asked.

Clue shrugged. "Same old same old, I guess." She paused before adding, "She did remember you coming over last night, though. Said you were a 'handsome young man.' And 'very sweet.'"

She made sure to set off "handsome young man" and "very sweet" with air quotes.

"That's great!" I said.

"Mhm. I thought you'd like that."

"No, I mean it's great that she remembered. That's a good thing, right?"

"Yeah," said Clue.

And that's all she said as we reached the underground tracks. The platform echoed with other commuters, their voices bouncing around the tiled walls. We found an empty bench between two yellow steel poles now polka dotted with colorful wads of gum. A florescent light buzzed above us.

"Can I ask you something?"

"Ugh," said Clue as she took a seat and stuffed her hands in her coat pockets. "Nothing good ever comes after that question." I don't know if she thought I was kidding, or if she hoped I'd just drop it, but eventually she conceded. "Sure."

"Why won't you let Rodney's parents help?"

The question had been burning inside me since the night before, when the three of us were huddled in Clue's smoky living room. Rodney had just made a suggestion, a pretty generous one, I thought, but it obviously struck a nerve.

231

Clue leaned back and sighed. "Because his mom is a *Real Housewives* wannabe? She'd buy us some frilly penthouse and drop us in the middle of Manhattan."

"Anddd...that's a bad thing?"

"What's with all the questions?" snapped Clue, leaning forward again. I instantly regretted bringing it back up. I'd scratched off a scab. Poured salt in an open wound. "What about you? You gonna tell me what happened to your face?"

There it was.

My eyes dropped to the space between us, tracing every heart and initial scratched into the bench. I'd wondered when she'd ask. The radios had been quiet all afternoon, which meant Rodney hadn't filled her in. He hadn't told her anything — about us rescuing the missing spikes *or* about me going all ninja in the ring.

"You wouldn't believe me if I told you."

Clue just rolled her eyes. So I told her. I told her everything. About the Lucky Duck Laundromat.

About Thad. The Mortal Kombat League. The oversized costume. My getting punched and kicked.

And of course about my winning.

After I finished, Clue crossed her arms and thought for a moment. She studied my face carefully, her eyes traveling over the bruise. Dissecting it piece by piece.

"Well, look at that," she said, half amused. "He climbs trees, *and* he kicks butt."

"Now it's your turn."

"You don't give up, do you, Farm Boy?"

I shrugged. "I just know you have a lot on your plate, and I'm sure it's exhausting. If someone wants to help, would it really be such a bad idea to at least consider it? Especially if it might be good for your mom?"

She stared at the wall of white tiles across the tracks.

"Clue?"

"No one can find out about her."

It all came out in one pent-up breath, one exhale, like she couldn't get the words off her chest fast enough. *No one can find out about her.*

"I know you know," she added. "I heard Rodney telling you." I expected her to be upset about Rodney sharing something so personal, but when she looked at me, her eyes held no anger. In fact, she was almost grinning. "Our apartment's the size of a matchbox. And Rodney has a big mouth."

The tension melted away between us after that, allowing Clue to finally breathe and talk and vent and feel and do whatever else she needed to do. I was just happy to listen. My dad always said, "The good Lord gave us one mouth and two ears for a reason." And now seemed as good a time as any to remember that.

"No one else can know about Mom," Clue repeated. "The second they do, they'll stick her in some treatment center or home, and I'll…" She shook her head and swallowed whatever emotion was threatening to bubble up. "They'll take her away," she whispered. "I know they will."

Jeez.

I thought waking up early on a Saturday morning to help Mom cater the Rotary Club's pancake breakfast was a pain. But that was nothing compared to what Clue was facing.

She'd *love* to help her mom cook.

She'd love her mom to be *able* to cook.

"She's slowly starting to forget everything," said Clue. "One day she's gonna wake up and not even know who I am. I know it sounds crazy, but I have to do whatever I can to make her remember. To keep me in her mind."

Like steal the star from the Rockefeller Center Christmas Tree, I thought.

Although I couldn't help but think there were plenty of easier — less criminal — ways to get someone's attention.

CHAPTER 41

It was already dark by the time the subway dropped us off at Herald Square, right next to Macy's department store. I'd never seen the place up close in person, but it was just as big as they say, gobbling up an entire city block.

"Whoa…"

My shoes rooted to the sidewalk as I stared. The word *Believe* glittered across the building's façade in a glowing script, and each window display along the store's street level was like a jewel box straight from Santa's Workshop.

Jewel box.

I'd have to remember that for a story sometime.

In typical Clue fashion, though, she somehow managed to zap every ounce of Christmas spirit in the air. "Ugh. Commercialism," she grumbled before moving on.

I followed, shaking my head and doing my best not to laugh.

Nine times out of ten, I've come to realize, New York City streets stink; it's just a fact. But at some point you start ignoring it all: the overflowing garbage bins, the cigarettes, the sewers, the tourist with horrible B.O. you get stuck behind at a crosswalk. As we turned the next corner, though, something smelled truly amazing — amazing enough to drown out the near-constant stench of weed.

"Hey!" I said, spotting the savory source.

It was a weenie stand, nothing special, just a silver cart plastered with laminated images of every kind of fried food imaginable. Steam poured from one of the vents.

I jogged over and stood under the cart's yellow and blue umbrella. "Want one?" I called back to Clue.

"Absolutely not."

"You sure? I bet they're delicioussss," I teased.

"I doubt itttt."

"Wait," I said in disbelief, freeing my hands from my pockets. "Have you never had one?" Clue remained silent. "You haven't, have you?"

She pointed her nose skyward and turned away. "I refuse to pay eight bucks for a tube of sketchy meat parts." She looked back over her shoulder, but when I didn't comment on her dramatics, she added, "It's highway robbery!"

I ordered two hotdogs with chili and mustard anyway and offered one to Clue.

"Robbery, huh? Sort of like stealing a star. Off the world's most famous Christmas tree?"

Clue rolled her eyes but took the dog. "Shut up."

CHAPTER 42

Waiting to go inside the Empire State Building was like waiting for a ride at Disney World. As we stood in line, tourists bundled up like Eskimos kept themselves busy by doing all the usual touristy things — taking family photos, livestreaming, and whatever else people do when they find themselves in the presence of a famous landmark. Me? I tried taking in the enormity of the skyscraper towering above us, and my neck about broke. The needle pierced through a layer of low-lying clouds, but even from some 1,400 feet away, you could still see it glowing through the mist.

"Coming?" said Clue. She'd finished her hotdog (which she thoroughly enjoyed, I might add) and was holding open one of the glass doors. When I caught up, she shook her head. "All of you writers and your *observing*."

She wasn't wrong.

I understood why so many of the greats flocked to New York, or at least set their stories here. The food, the lights, the views, the almost constant sense of adventure — it was inspiring. The perfect playground for a writer and his band of characters.

Gold and silver garland decorated the Empire State Building's marble lobby, and a pianist played Christmas carols on a gleaming baby grand piano. Definitely a different vibe from the first time I'd visited.

It was the summer we moved Aunt Celeste into her apartment, and Mom, still upset about her baby sister's "life choices," was ready to get out of the city ASAP. Which meant everyone had to listen to her rehash the whole thing over and over again.

When is that girl going to grow up?

What about medical care? A 401(k)? Benefits!

Did you see the eyeroll when I mentioned the cost of living up here?

I just don't know what she's thinking....

Somehow, in the midst of Mom's venting sessions, I'd convinced her and Dad to take us up to the observation deck on the eighty-sixth floor before we left.

Mom hated the wind.

And now I was back, hoping for a better experience with Clue.

I scanned our tickets with my phone, and then we headed straight for the elevator. Luckily, no one rolled in behind us, so we didn't have to ride with a bunch of strangers and awkwardly stare at the walls to avoid eye contact. The elevator pulled us up floor by floor, shooting us farther into the clouds. My excitement grew with each level.

I really wanted Clue to love it. Or, at least not hate it. She wasn't exactly the kind of girl who gushed over things and hugged you to death, but I hoped it would at least put a smile on her face.

The numbers clicked higher and higher.

98

99

100

101

Ding!

The elevator slowed to a stop with a tiny rumble. "Welcome to the one hundred-second floor," said a slightly robotic female voice.

And then the doors slid open.

CHAPTER 43

"Are you kidding me?"

I didn't even have to look at her; I could hear the amazement in Clue's voice.

I motioned for her to go first, and she slowly stepped out into the dim, circular room, her eyes swiping from side to side. Soaking it all in. I'd never been up this high, but the walls were floor-to-ceiling glass — just like the website had promised — offering a complete, unobstructed 360-degree view of Manhattan.

But no website could have done it justice.

This was the magic of New York City.

This view. This moment.

Apart from an Asian family of three and an elderly couple whispering off to the left, we had the whole place pretty much to ourselves. Which was insane. The observatory was dark enough and large enough that we felt alone, just the two of us, hovering above the City That Never Sleeps.

It felt like we were on top of the world.

Buildings and skyscrapers twinkled as far as the eye could see, resembling a stacked city of glowing Legos. You could even see the ice rink at Bryant Park from this angle. I was tempted to whip out my phone and snap some photos for Rodney, but I was more interested in watching Clue. She moved toward the room's curved edge and pressed her hands against the glass.

"What do you think?" I asked.

"I…"

Her voice sounded small — especially for someone like Cluenette Perez.

"I've never seen anything like it," she whispered. "This view. I've never been up this high." She shook her head, taking it all in. "I had no idea…."

I dared to move a little closer. Tiny pockets of purple lights dotted the ceiling, casting an almost underwater glow around the room, so it somehow felt safe standing shoulder to shoulder in the darkness.

"Well," I said, "if you're going to design buildings one day, I figured you should see all of your competition first."

The glass in front of Clue's face fogged as she exhaled. "Thank you."

And suddenly it was all worth it. Bringing her up here, spending some of that all too precious dog-walking money, getting her out of the apartment — it was worth it. Because Clue was smiling. She was actually enjoying herself.

"I've walked by this building my entire life…and never knew what I was missing until now. Thank you," she whispered again.

"Of course."

"I'm gonna design one of these someday," she said, marveling at every skyscraper around us. Some were so close that you could see people through the yellow window blocks, cooking dinner or wrapping up last-minute paperwork at the office. "I'm gonna design it and see the whole thing through. Start to finish."

"I believe it."

"But it'll be affordable for people," she added. "So you don't have to own Instagram or sell buckets of drugs to live there."

My shoulders jumped a little, but I forced myself not to laugh out loud. "Do people sell buckets of drugs?" I asked.

And right there in the shadows — maybe because it was so quiet above the City That Never Sleeps, maybe because everything felt safer in the near-darkness — Clue nudged me in the arm.

"You know what I mean."

CHAPTER 44

We caught up with Rodney at the Channel Gardens as planned; I guess the angels had become a sort of good luck charm. When he saw us coming, he quickly angled his camera toward the sky and started frantically looking through the lens like it was a telescope.

"Rodney," said Clue, "what are you doing?"

He let the camera fall to his chest. "It's 7:02," he announced, rolling up a coat sleeve and tapping his rubber watch, which looked like some goofy *Spy Kids* prop. "You're late!"

"Why are you shooting the sky?" I asked. "Isn't it kind of hard to see the stars from the city?"

Rodney clapped me on the back and laughed. "No, mate. I was looking for flying pigs!" He tossed his other arm across Clue's shoulders, so he was sandwiched between us. "This one's *never* late."

Clue shrugged off his embrace. "Can we just get going?"

Rodney straightened his back and threw up a salute. "Aye aye, captain."

The "going" proved to be short-lived that night. After weaving through the crowds, we reached the other side of Rockefeller Center's ice rink — but we weren't the only ones in need of the Christmas tree.

"You've got to be kidding me," said Clue, stopping short.

Rodney scratched his beanie like he had some serious scalp itch. Or maybe he was just confused like the rest of us. "What's going on? What is all this?"

"Well," said Clue, crossing her arms, examining the area, "I think Hallmark beat us to it. Looks like they're shooting scenes for one of their lame Christmas movies or something."

She wasn't wrong. The purple Hallmark crown shimmered on the side of a nearby trailer. Crew members scurried around with their headsets and clipboards, while others adjusted boom mics and camera equipment. And the amount of cord snaking along the pavement was probably enough to wrap around the entire planet. Maybe twice.

"Crikey," said Rodney. "Do you think Lacey Chabert's in this one?" He craned his neck this way and that, trying to catch a glimpse of his apparent celebrity crush.

"Great," said Clue, too annoyed to pay Rodney any mind. "Of all nights, they had to pick *tonight*? We have *stuff* to do. The tree's not even lit," she pointed out. "Why would they film before the ceremony?"

"Let's just hope it's *only* tonight," I said.

Rodney shrugged and stole a few steps toward the set. When he turned around to face us again, a hopeful gleam twinkled in his eyes. "Perhaps...we could still get the job done?"

"Rodney," said Clue. "You're not meeting Lacey."

"I'm not talking about Lacey," he groaned, throwing his head back. "I mean, what if we're just extra careful?"

Clue and I looked at each other. All we could do was blink.

Was he serious?

"Of course," she finally said. "Why didn't I think of that? I'm sure the hundreds of crew members crawling around this place won't notice a couple of teens scrambling up the tree. Maybe we'll even be in a few shots?"

Rodney nodded excitedly, but then his face fell as he caught on. "You're right," he mumbled. "Dumb idea."

Clue shed her beanie and wiped her forehead. "Okay," she sighed, pulling the hat back over her ears. "Plan B. I guess we'll just have to get twice as many spikes tomorrow."

Which didn't sound the least bit appealing to anyone.

Most of all me.

CHAPTER 45

Aunt Celeste was back from rehearsal by the time I returned to the apartment, but she was already zonked out on the couch, a cup of cold tea on the coffee table next to her pink-socked feet. Gerdy lifted her head from the rug when I walked in. Her jaw twisted in circles as she chewed on something that was probably bad for her, but I didn't bother to investigate.

"I'm home," I announced quietly, sinking into the recliner.

The lights were off, but the TV was still going. I grabbed a handful of chips from the bowl in Aunt Celeste's arms and made myself comfortable just as the dramatic intro of some kind of breaking news flashed across the screen.

"I'm here at Rockefeller Center," the blonde reporter began, "where the renowned ice-skating rink has become more of a pond over the last hour."

The broadcast cut to a second camera and zoomed in on the ice rink. The reporter was right —

the ice was gone. Instead, people were staggering through a large pool of slush, wobbling as best they could to reach the steps in their skates.

I stopped chewing and leaned forward in disbelief.

"Officials are still trying to figure out how the cooling system malfunctioned," the reporter said. "But, according to Rockefeller Center maintenance, the problem is already being addressed, and the rink should be up and running for skaters by tomorrow morning. For MBN News, I'm Meghan Palladino."

She's brilliant, I thought.

Not Meghan. *Clue.* This had her name written all over it. First the smoke bomb, then the giant kangaroo float, and now this. Another brilliant distraction, even if it was a wasted one.

I couldn't begin to understand how she'd pulled it off — how she had *time* to pull it off — but it was too much of a coincidence to not be her brainchild.

I found the remote wedged between a sofa cushion and turned off the TV.

Usually I was exhausted when I returned to the apartment. You know, from climbing nearly seventy feet of branches, dismantling a 300-pound star, and enduring hours of gut-wrenching anxiety from worrying that we'd eventually get caught and be shipped off to juvie.

But tonight was different. Tonight was easy. Even kind of *fun*.

Just a New York hotdog and a trip to the Empire State Building with Clue.

Since every joint and bone in my body didn't feel like it had been beaten with a sledgehammer, I actually had enough energy to write. I felt creative. Inspired. So, I pulled the chain on the lamp next to the recliner, gave Gerdy a good scratch under her fuzzy chin, and as Aunt Celeste dreamed away, I opened my notebook and got to work.

CHAPTER 46

Rodney sounded exactly like Squidward when he radioed in the next morning. If Squidward was Australian. And suffering a terrible head cold.

"Mates?" His nasally voice crackled through the speaker. "Come in, mates."

Clue reached her radio before I could even pry myself from the recliner. "Hey. You sound horrible."

A very Clue-like good morning.

"I'm completely kna—*knackered*," said Rodney, just as he released another sneeze. "I spent all last night breathing through my mouth, so I didn't get much sleep."

"I fall into a freezing pond, but you're the one who gets sick?" I could practically see Clue shaking her head. "Good thing school's cancelled, I guess."

"School is closed today?" I said, finally conscious enough to string words together.

"Have you looked outside, mate?"

I hadn't. But I should've known. The apartment was glowing with that special kind of blinding light that only comes from one thing. I shuffled over to the living room window, and sure enough, a couple inches of snow covered balcony railings, parked cars, trash bins, and the few trees lining the street below.

I pressed the button on my radio. "I didn't know it was calling for snow."

"No one did," said Clue. "The pipes at school froze over last night and burst. Or something like that."

After talking with Clue and Rodney, I found Aunt Celeste in the kitchen, where she was racing around trying to make sure Gerdy was settled for the day while also globbing on some hideous shade of orange lipstick.

"I'm late late *late*," she announced, smacking her lips and tossing the lipstick tube in her purse. "Good morning, d— *what on earth?*" She'd caught sight of my face. Before I even had a chance to open my mouth, she rushed over to examine the bruise more closely, gently running her fingers over the sore skin. "Nate, what happened?"

"You don't want to know."

"Did those friends of yours do this? The one with the trash bag and that whole dump truck fiasco?"

"No," I assured her. "Really, I'm fine. I just had a little...accident." Which was the best I could do at 7 a.m.

Aunt Celeste sighed and took one last grimacing look at the bruise. "Your mother is going to kill me when she sees this."

"I'll make sure she knows it has nothing to do with your impeccable capabilities as a caretaker. Or lack of," I added with a smirk.

"See that you do," said Aunt Celeste, pointing, as I backstepped to the counter and poured myself a cup of coffee. "You wayward nephew of mine."

I added creamer and took a sip. "Is there anywhere to buy a Christmas tree around here?"

Aunt Celeste loved Christmas almost as much as she loved the theater. "My *tree*," she'd gushed when I'd first arrived last week. "Look at my *tree*!"

It was bubblegum-pink and, according to her, had been fully decorated and displayed since Halloween. Colorful ornaments crowded every branch, ranging from tiny performing arts masks to porcelain playbills to a weird assortment of sweets, like plastic lollipops and ice cream cones. Of course, to top it all off, everything was doused with a gallon of glitter.

Aunt Celeste considered it festive. Mom would call it gaudy.

"Of course! Mr. O'Connell on the next street over. I think that's his name," Aunt Celeste said, checking her blue curls in the mirror one last time before heading out the door. "Sweet older gentleman. I bought one from him my first Christmas here, you know. Before I found *that* beauty on sale after the holidays." She nodded toward the explosion of pink in the corner of the living room. "Why do you ask?"

"Just wondering," I shrugged. "Good luck in rehearsal."

Rule Number One when traveling to New York in winter: Always bring boots. Just in case.

Five minutes in the snow with my paper-thin Chucks and my socks were already soggy, like I was dumpster-diving all over again. Oh, well. I'd spent most of my extra cash on tickets to the Empire State Building, so I'd just have to deal with wet feet. I gripped the straps of my backpack and kept moving.

Sure enough, on the very next street, I found an elderly man with a bushy gray beard sitting under a wooden lean-to on the sidewalk. A row of Christmas trees lined the pavement next to him.

"Mr. O'Connell?"

"That would be me," he said, rocking forward. He kept his mittened hands wrapped tightly around himself. "What can I do for you?"

"I'm looking for a Christmas tree — but nothing huge. Just something really small, if you have it."

Mr. O'Connell looked down the row of trees and shook his head. "I'm afraid the smallest I've got is a couple of seven-footers."

"Oh." My mind went to the room, to the ceiling and floor space, and I knew even without measuring that it wouldn't work. "That's okay," I said, turning. "Thank you, anyway."

"I tell you what," said Mr. O'Connell. He rose from his chair, slowly straightening out his knees and back. "How about we take a look at this one over here and see if we can figure something out."

He motioned me on, so I followed him to the very last tree at the end of the line.

"She's what some people might call a Charlie Brown tree." The grin beneath his beard squished even more wrinkles onto his face. "Not the prettiest thing," he said, "but she might do."

Mr. O'Connell was right — the tree wasn't hitting on much. The branches were so sparse that you could see clean through to the trunk, and the few needles still holding on for dear life weren't even that green. More of a puke color than anything else. But a Charlie Brown tree was better than nothing.

"If it was about half that size, it'd be perfect," I said.

Mr. O'Connell raised a hand and then limped back to his hut. He returned with a rusted hand saw, winked, and said, "I think we can make that happen."

I leaned the tree over so Mr. O'Connell could cut. He removed his mittens and got to work, and within seconds, I had a perfect three-foot tree.

"Thank you, sir."

"My pleasure," said Mr. O'Connell. "I hope you and your family enjoy."

"Actually, it's for a friend of mine," I said, digging out some money from my wallet.

"That's mighty kind of you." His eyes twinkled like a proud grandfather. When I offered him the cash, he held up a hand. "This one's on me," he said quietly. "Tell your friend to have a Merry Christmas."

CHAPTER 47

I found the apartment building easily enough. It wasn't until I started walking up the stairs to the third floor, though, dragging the top of the once-seven-foot tree behind me, that my stomach began turning inside out.

Why was I suddenly so nervous? I'd been to Clue's place before, and her mom was probably the sweetest lady on earth. Plus, there was no smoke in the air this time, which meant one less thing to worry about.

Still.

It took a while for anyone to answer the door. Actually, it probably wasn't long at all. Probably just my nerves lying to me. I was torn between leaving and knocking again, but my decision was made for me when the door creaked open. And there was Clue — although it looked nothing like her.

Instead of the usual overalls, combat boots, and black beanie, she was wearing sweatpants and an oversized Pokémon T-shirt. She'd piled her dark hair into a messy bun.

"Hey," she said, looking a little confused.

"Hey." I cleared my throat and could feel my face burning. This was Clue. Relaxed, comfortable, down-to-earth Clue.

And she looked beautiful.

"Nice socks," I said, noticing the sleeping sloths.

She fidgeted, resting one heel on the other ankle as she leaned against the doorframe and crossed her arms. "What are you doing here?"

I stood the tree in front of me and grinned. "You've got a snow day," I shrugged. "That's the perfect time to decorate a Christmas tree, right?"

The surprise (maybe shock?) was written all over her face, and at first I couldn't tell if it was a good or bad thing. For a moment, I thought she might even ask me to take it back. Maybe I'd overstepped some boundary.

But then Mrs. Perez shuffled into view behind her.

"A tree!" she gushed, and the smile on her face was priceless. "How thoughtful."

Clue's confusion melted into the smallest grin. She nodded and opened the door wide, stepping aside for me to come in.

"You didn't have to do that," she whispered.

I winked and carried the tree inside.

Since I'd bought the world's smallest Christmas tree, we set it on top of the sofa's end table. Clue dragged out an old box of decorations from the hallway closet, and we got to work decorating, first with lights and then the ornaments. They all seemed to be homemade too. A far cry from Aunt Celeste's plastic produce.

"Is this you?" I asked, holding up a nutcracker made of green and yellow felt. A school photo was glued down where its face should've been; the little girl appeared to be seven or eight.

"You can leave that one in the box," said Clue.

Mrs. Perez took the photo and studied it closely. "Absolutely not," she said, smiling. *Remembering.* "You're missing your two front teeth here."

"Thanks, Mom."

But Mrs. Perez paid her no mind. She clutched the ornament to her chest and carried it over to the tree like it was as fragile as glass. "Front and center," she said, hanging it on one of the few flimsy branches.

No matter how embarrassing (or sometimes ugly) the ornaments were, the two of them loved digging through the box and reliving old memories. Angels made from bits of lace...stars covered in stickers and gold glitter...construction paper candy canes... Each one was like a forgotten treasure.

I sat down on the couch for a bit while they finished decorating. Mrs. Perez seemed to be doing well today, so I wanted to give them their space.

Plus, I had an image burning in my mind that I had to get down on paper.

CHAPTER 48

"Nate?"

I looked up from the notebook, startled. "Huh?"

"What do you think?"

Clue motioned to the tree. Mrs. Perez was beaming, hands to her chest again.

"It looks *great*," I said, getting up to admire their handiwork. It wasn't until then that I noticed the star on top. Each side was made from a small piece of sheet metal, perfectly buffed and polished, and every angle had been welded together perfectly. Pinpricked holes dotted the entire star, allowing the extra tree lights that had been stuffed inside to shine through and cast glowing orbs around the room. "This is incredible," I said, touching one of the star's silvery points.

Clue came over and stood next to me. "My dad made that," she said. "He always had extra stuff lying around the shop. He could take anything and make it look like a million bucks."

"No kidding."

"Cocoa?" said Mrs. Perez, shuffling off into the kitchen in her bedroom slippers.

Clue trailed after her. "I can do that, Mom."

"No, no. You sit and talk to your friend. I think I can manage some hot chocolate."

Clue wasn't convinced — and neither was I, not after the toast disaster — but we sat down on the couch anyway. At least we'd be nearby if the microwave exploded or something.

Neither of us said anything for a good thirty seconds. That might not sound like much, but if you've ever had to give a class speech at school, you know. Time does you dirty. Two minutes can feel like eternity.

It's not that I didn't have anything to say. Actually, it was the complete opposite. Sitting there next to Clue, close enough to even smell her shampoo, I had so many things I wanted to get off my chest. But choosing one seemed impossible. Thankfully, the old record player in the corner was still playing one last carol to cushion the silence between us. Some soft, scratchy version of "Silent Night."

Finally, somewhere in the middle of verse three, Clue's voice broke.

"That was really thoughtful of you," she whispered. "Bringing the tree and everything. I think Mom needed it just as much as I did."

"Everyone needs a little Christmas cheer," I said, shrugging.

Clue sort of grinned and played with the fingers in her lap. Then, she looked up and stared at the tiny tree, her face glowing in its twinkling light. "Christmas was my dad's favorite. We never had much, but…he always made sure we had a tree." She nodded toward the record player. "Those were his. Bing Crosby. Frank Sinatra. He made sure this place was *filled* with Christmas music this time of year. He loved it."

She took a deep breath, giving in to thoughts of her dad. Allowing his memory to wash over her.

"I really am sorry if my bringing the tree over was too much. I just thought y'all might enjoy it."

"No, it's fine," said Clue, pulling her legs up on the couch and wrapping her arms around her knees. "Really." She kept her eyes glued to the tree. "When dad left…it's like he took Christmas with him. I didn't want a tree because it reminded me of him."

"I'm sorry…." It's all I could think to say.

Clue shook her head and wiped a stray tear with the neck of her T-shirt. "Don't be," she whispered. Her voice was suddenly very hoarse. "There hasn't been much time to think about a tree these past few Christmases, anyway."

In that moment, I realized what was happening. Walls were crumbling, and Clue was crawling out from behind the stone-hard façade she'd built for herself. I could feel it. I could hear it in her voice.

She was more than some girl with a knack for breaking the rules.

She was more than the black clothes and boots and eye rolling.

She was a girl in *pain*.

"It's okay to think about yourself sometimes too, you know."

And then, no matter if she slapped me right across the face, I had to do it this time. I had to hold her hand.

To my relief, she didn't pull away. She didn't even flinch. More tears immediately filled her eyes, and I knew, deep down, that Clue needed to hear those words.

"You're the best daughter a mom could have," I said, giving her hand a squeeze. "She's lucky to have you."

"Cocoa?"

Mrs. Perez had returned, rattling a tray of three steaming mugs as she stood there in her slippers. I quickly let go of Clue's hand and put a couple more inches between us.

Suddenly, the apartment felt like a hundred degrees.

CHAPTER 49

We sat on the couch talking and sipping hot chocolate for the next hour or so. I'd tell a funny story from back home, and then Clue would share one from her childhood. Like the time her dad fixed a customer's car, handed him the keys, and walked away. The customer slid into the driver's seat of his old sedan — only to find five-year-old Clue sitting cross-legged in the passenger seat, grinning ear to ear.

"Remember that, Mom?" asked Clue. "I almost went home with a *stranger*."

Mrs. Perez nodded, but judging from the faraway look in her eyes, it was obvious she didn't. Either that or she was just getting tired.

"I'd better go," I said, setting my empty mug on the tray resting on the coffee table. "Thanks again for the hot chocolate, Mrs. Perez. It was delicious."

She remained seated in the armchair. "Of course," she waved groggily. "Thank *you* for the beautiful tree, N...N..." Her brow furrowed as she searched for my name.

"Nate," said Clue.

"Nate," said Mrs. Perez, smiling blankly again.

Clue followed me to the door and thanked me for coming over. I stepped out onto the landing, but before we parted, she pressed something crisp into my hand.

It was a yellow sticky note, folded several times over into a tiny yellow square. I opened it as I made my way down the stairs:

Subway station on 36th @ 5 p.m.

If you can.

– C

Five o'clock came, and as I rounded the corner of the deli, there was Clue, one stoplight over, rounding her own corner. We crossed the street and met at the subway entrance.

"I think this is becoming our thing," I joked.

"I guess so." Clue kept dodging my eyes. She stared at my chest instead, almost as if she were embarrassed. About her mom? Or the fact that she'd asked me to meet her? I wasn't sure. "Glad you could make it," she said.

We were back to our usual attire, buried beneath black coats, beanies, and of course Clue's trusty overalls. Seeing us in our dark clothes, I suddenly remembered the task ahead...and the fact that Rodney was probably still sneezing his brains out and wouldn't be joining us.

But it was a three-man job.

What are we going to do?

I pushed the thought away for the time being and followed Clue below ground.

"So, what's going on?"

Clue glanced over her shoulder and shrugged mischievously, already falling back into old habits. "You'll see."

When we emerged from underground, the night air hit us like a cold shower. Icy wind whipped between buildings and blasted our faces as we dodged piles of dirty snow crowding the sidewalks.

It was the kind of cold that would've been miserable anywhere else besides New York.

Because in New York — especially at Christmastime — there are too many sights to keep you distracted from trivial inconveniences like numb noses and frostbitten toes.

Like Bryant Park.

I thought maybe Clue was taking me there because it seemed like the place to be. People laughing and guzzling down thick, steamy cocoa. Pop-up shops with every kind of souvenir you could imagine. Ice skating. Music. Fried food on a stick.

But Clue kept walking. "This way," she said, leading us around the park.

By the time we reached the corner of the block, I knew exactly where she was taking me; it was hands down my favorite building in New York. But...how did she know? Instead of gleaming steel and precision-cut glass, this place held its own in the middle of Manhattan with its thick blocks of gray-veined marble, like some sort of ancient temple. Almost as if the Greek gods had designed it themselves.

In that moment, even a free trip to Disney wouldn't have compared. We stepped closer, and I couldn't help but smile at all the things I'd only seen through a computer screen: the two stone lions, the marble pillars, the arches that framed the grand entrance.

Clue was taking me to the New York Public Library.

CHAPTER 50

It started snowing again as we made our way toward the stone steps. Like the previous night's storm was coughing up just a few more flurries. I convinced Clue to take a selfie with me in front of one of the lions — Fortitude, I think — and then we began climbing the stairs.

Clue kept glancing down at my grungy Converses, a far cry from her thick combat boots with enough rubber on the soles to replace about a dozen tires.

"Would you stop judging me already?" I was trying my best to tread over the frozen puddles.

"I haven't said a word!"

"Trust me," I said, practically doing a full-on split as I stretched and streeeetched to skip two icy steps. My feet stuck the landing. "Your silence says it all."

We conquered the stairs without any mishaps, and once we reached the top, the treacherous climb proved to be worth it. Because stepping through the library's giant bronze doors was like walking into a legit castle.

"Whoa," I said, coming face to face with the second biggest Christmas tree I'd ever seen. It was the perfect shape, like a green upside-down ice cream cone. A ring of bright red poinsettias surrounded the base.

Clue nodded next to me. "Not bad, huh?"

We stood in the middle of the marble entry hall, my eyes darting everywhere. It was hard to know where to look first. Clicking footsteps echoed around the cavernous room as people trekked up and down the two grand staircases and disappeared through curved archways. They all seemed to know where they were going. But I didn't have a clue.

"Come on."

Clue veered to the left, so I followed. After a bajillion steps, we finally reached the third floor, stopping in something called the McGraw Rotunda. Dark, gleaming wood covered the walls, and a strange mural of naked people splashed across the vaulted ceiling. One guy was throwing a spear; another hugged what looked like a dead tree.

Clue led the way through two more sets of heavy wooden doors. She nodded at the staff in their crisp white shirts as we passed, and they smiled back in such a friendly way that made me think this wasn't Clue's first venture into the library.

"Hey, Viv," she said, addressing a plump lady sitting behind the circulation desk.

So she was *a regular.*

I'd known her less than a week, but Clue definitely didn't strike me as the type of girl who sat quietly in the stacks reading Shakespeare. I was impressed.

Viv peered over her purple-rimmed glasses. "Well, if it isn't my favorite patron." Her voice was soft, clear, and story-like. If she ever grew tired of all the marble, I was sure she could narrate audiobooks for a living. Viv reached across her keyboard to squeeze Clue's hand, her bracelets jangling, and then she looked my way, smiling. "And who is this handsome young man?"

"Oh. Right." Clue nodded the way you nod when you're trying to rattle your brain. The classic buy-yourself-more-time nod. I knew it well. "Nate, this is Mrs. Vivian Castleberry. The *best* librarian in the city. Viv, this is Nate." She swallowed. Hard. "He's...he..."

Viv's eyebrows kept inching higher and higher, and her mouth dropped open like a fish, like she would gladly help finish the sentence if she knew where it was going.

"We're friends," I said, stepping forward to shake Viv's hand. I smiled. The word didn't taste quite as weird on my tongue that time. "Nice to meet you."

"Friends..." Viv drew out the word extra slowly, and she didn't seem to want to let go of my hand. "Lovely," she said, shooting Clue a dramatic wink.

Clue rolled her eyes, and Viv started giggling, waving the whole thing off. She was like the Clue Version of Aunt Celeste. Maybe everybody had one.

"Please just tell me we haven't missed it," said Clue, trying to resist the grin pulling on her cheeks.

Viv finished dabbing her eyes with a tissue and slid on her purple frames again. "Of course not. These things never start on time. He just got started about ten minutes ago." She nodded toward an open doorway to her right. "Go on. There are still a few empty seats."

"Thank you."

Viv winked again as we passed. *"Pleasure to meet you, Nateee."*

CHAPTER 51

The library back in Shady Springs was less a public library and more of a book graveyard. The rickety blue shelves, already half empty, became even more pathetic at the end of every year, when the librarians discarded cartloads of books due to "lack of use." In fact, I'm pretty sure those shelves held more dust bunnies than novels.

Which made sense. I'd been going there before I could even read, back when I was just a chubby toddler visiting on weekends with Mom. A lot of Saturdays had passed since then...and I was *convinced* that I was the one and only patron.

Needless to say, Shady Springs was the sort of place books went to die.

But not here. Not in the Rose Main Reading Room.

Just imagine the Great Hall at Hogwarts, fill it with books, and you've got the right vibe.

"Over here," whispered Clue as we tiptoed to our seats in the very back of the room.

"Hang on…."

I froze before sitting, suddenly recognizing the speaker that Viv had mentioned. He was tall and lanky, probably around my parents' age, and rocking an impressively thick black beard. Honestly, with the black suit and long face, he was a dead ringer for Abe Lincoln. All he needed was the top hat.

"Hey," said Clue. "You good?"

"That's Augustine Grant," I said, pointing. Apparently trying to convince myself. "He's one of the greatest writers of literary fiction working right now. *We're All Matchsticks. House Under a Raging Sea.* Every single thing he puts out is a masterpiece."

Clue made a soft choking sound. *"Augustine?"* she scoffed. "For real? What kind of name is Augusti—?"

She stopped when she saw my raised eyebrows, a not-so-subtle reminder of her own unique title.

"I mean...Augustine?" She leaned back in her chair. "*Beautiful* name. Love it."

Augustine's deep voice reverberated off the tile floor as the audience leaned in to catch every word. Normally I would've done the same. I mean, his career was the kind that writers dream about — millions of copies sold, dozens of language translations, several film deals — but the Rose Main Reading Room had already captured my attention. I'd practically drooled over images of the place, and now here I was. Sitting under the glow of the sparkling chandeliers. Staring up at the gilded ceiling's ornate carvings. Studying the murals of orange and pink clouds caught mid-sunset.

As Augustine Grant's speech played in the background, I breathed in the smell of paper and lemon wood polish and well-worn books.

It was all thanks to Clue.

"You knew about this?"

"I saw it on a notice board last week." She shrugged. "If you're gonna be some big-time author, I figured you should see how a reading's

284

done. Who knows. Maybe you'll be reading your own book here someday."

Just then, another change rippled between us. Another thread sewn. Another stone added. It was as thin as a sheet of paper — but still. I could feel it. A shimmer of something new.

"Plus, you took me to the Empire State Building," she whispered. "I owed you one."

"You're not going soft on me now, are you?" I teased, bumping her with my elbow. Because I was still picturing her in those sweats and baggy T-shirt curled up on the living room couch. That was her, I thought, and *that* Clue was the kind of person — friend, even — who wouldn't mind an elbow bump.

Of course, Clue was nothing if not determined. Instead of pushing back, she kept her focus zeroed in on Augustine Grant, like she was suddenly his biggest fan and had personally been enlightened by his twenty-three published works.

But the smile in her cheek gave her away.

CHAPTER 52

We still had some time to kill after the reading, so Clue followed me up to the wrap-around mezzanine while I roamed the shelves. I could've wasted hours checking out the leather and canvas spines up there, but I knew it was getting late. I knew that soon we'd be stepping outside to brave the cold again, hiking toward Rockefeller Center for the very last time. And once that thought entered my brain, it stuck.

Because tomorrow was the tree lighting ceremony.

Tomorrow the entire country would be watching.

Tomorrow everyone would see what we had done.

"Are you sure this is a good idea?"

Clue reshelved the book she was holding. "What do you mean?"

I couldn't help it. Now that we were about to cross the finish line, I was reminded of just how badly I never wanted to run this race.

"It just seems like everything's falling apart," I said. "The tree's covered in snow. Rodney can't help because he's sick. And we have to get twice as many spikes tonight." I released a much-needed breath. "Maybe it's a sign."

"Come on," said Clue. "You're not chickening out on me now, are you?"

"I'm just saying...we're sort of at a disadvantage here."

Clue stepped away and looked out over the mezzanine balcony. Her eyes scanned the room below as the staff wiped tables and picked up empty water bottles. "You don't get it, Nate," she said finally, shaking her head. "Your family's *obsessed* with you. Sure, it's annoying when they're all up in your business or texting you nonstop. But at least they care." She paused before adding quietly, "My dad hasn't spoken to me in four years."

I posted up beside her, unsure of what to say.

"He took off the day after my twelfth birthday party to go chase his big break. Just like that. He left everything behind — the shop, his tools. Me. Mom. One minute he was there…and the next he wasn't."

I couldn't even pretend to understand. My folks were the definition of "helicopter parents." Look it up in Webster's, and you'll definitely find their photos smiling back at you. Case in point: When I first got my cellphone, they wanted me to immediately set up the tracker app, some nonsense the sales guy was going on about. So I may or may not have played the technologically-challenged card. I wasn't a rebel or anything, but the thought of my parents sitting on the couch with a bowl of greasy popcorn watching my every move gave me the creeps.

"I'm glad you've at least got your mom," I said. "You two seem really close."

As soon as I saw Clue's reaction, though, I regretted opening my big mouth. Her eyes filled with tears, and she had to look up to keep them from running.

"Pretty soon Mom won't even remember she has a daughter. It's like I won't even exist at that point." Her white knuckles gripped the banister. "That's why I have to do this."

Clue thought long and hard before she spoke again. Squeaky shoes down below filled the silence, accompanied by the occasional spray of disinfectant. Clue needed time, and I understood that. It's not every day you air out your family's personal business — especially to some random guy you threatened out on the ice only days before.

When she was good and ready, she said, "New York will remember me. Even if my own family doesn't. *I'll finally be somebody that people don't forget.*"

A sting hit my own eyes without warning. Because beneath it all, that was the sad truth. Beneath the overalls and the scheming and the planning, the confidence and all the rough edges, that's how Clue really saw herself. *Forgettable.*

I blinked away the burn, scrambling to find the right words.

"You already *are* that person," I said. "To Rodney. To Viv... To me." I rapped my knuckles against the cold railing. "Trust me," I smiled. "When someone forces you to break the law and risk your life climbing up a tree, they're pretty hard to forget."

Clue shook her head, wiping away whatever had escaped down her cheek. "I have to do this," she said matter-of-factly. "And I can't do it without you." She brushed away more tears, turned to me, and nodded. The smallest grin tugged at her perfect lips, like she was no longer forcing me to make a decision but encouraging me to side with her. As an ally. "Are you in?"

My heart didn't really give me a choice, especially with those big brown eyes looking at me like that. So I nodded.

Of course I was.

CHAPTER 53

We reached Rockefeller Center at *seven o'clock sharp*, just as Clue liked. The place, as always, was crawling with tourists, and sure enough, there was the tree, a thin layer of powdery snow coating each branch. There was the ice rink, completely solid and skateable once again. And there was Rodney, waving goofily at every pretty girl who passed by.

Wait — *Rodney?*

He caught sight of Clue and me rushing over. "Reporting for duty, mates!" he said, throwing up a salute. He tried rapping a few bars for us, but it quickly dissolved into a bunch of coughing and hacking.

"What are you doing here, man?" I said. "I thought you were at home sick?"

"Oh, I'm still sick," he mumbled.

That much was clear, judging from the wad of tissue stuffed in each nostril. He'd even left behind his camera tonight, and in its place was a box of Puffs Plus Lotion that he'd somehow fastened to his camera strap for easy access.

"But," he continued nasally, "like I always say, a soldier *never* leaves his troop behind."

He sneezed, shooting both pieces of tissue onto the pavement.

"Okay, okay," said Clue, patting his shoulder. "Let's get this show on the road before you cough up a lung. Is the distraction ready?"

"Diiiistraction...?" Rodney finished re-plugging his nose with tissues. "What distraction?"

Clue laughed and gave him a friendly nudge in the arm. But instead of joining her, Rodney just blinked, his eyes roaming between the two of us.

"You're joking, right?" said Clue, her face hardening like a tub of old Play-Doh. Rodney's blank expression proved he wasn't. "You were supposed to handle tonight's distraction! I had the ice rink yesterday, remember? I thought you had it covered!"

Though she probably wanted to scream, throw her beanie to the ground, and stomp on it, Clue took one long breath and just walked away.

"I'm sorry!" Rodney called after her. "I forgot, okay? I've been a bit under the weather, you know."

Looks like we're not finishing the job after all, I thought.

I'd be lying if I said I wasn't somewhat relieved. The night was growing colder with every minute that passed, and the idea of cozying up on Aunt Celeste's couch with a cup of hot chocolate and my notebook was sounding better and better. I stuffed my hands inside the fleece lining of my coat pockets to keep them warm — and my fingertips bumped into something thin and crisp.

Thad's business card.

I pulled it out and read over the whole thing once again. I couldn't keep from smiling at the cheesiness of it all. I pictured big, hulking Thad hunched over some ancient computer, his massive legs stuffed under the tiniest desk. I imagined him typing one keystroke at a time, nodding his own approval, believing this card held the same quality as that of some famous lawyer or big-time film producer.

Cheesy or not, a lightbulb went off.

You need anything, just let me know. That's what he'd said.

"Hang on," I said, reaching for my cell phone. Clue rejoined us just as I was punching in Thad's number.

"What is it?" she asked.

You need anything, just let me know.

I held the phone up to my ear and silently prayed that my fellow League member would answer. "I think I might have us a distraction."

CHAPTER 54

Luckily, Thad and some of the other League members were having dinner in Midtown, just a few blocks away.

"Theirshrimplinguineisthe*best*," Thad garbled through a mouthful of pasta. I could hear music and dishes clinking in the background.

"That's great," I said. "Uh, listen, Thad. Remember giving me your business card? And telling me to call if I needed anything?"

I left out the part about my leading his team to victory — pure luck or not — but I was fully prepared to bring it up if need be.

"Of course I do, little dude," Thad said between chews. "We'd be a bunch of losers if it wasn't for you. What's up? You ready to get back in the ring?"

"No," I said, probably too quickly. The idea of drowning in another oversized Halloween costume while swinging yet another toy weapon was enough to keep me away forever. "No, I'm good."

Clue and Rodney pressed in around me. Clue tapped her wrist, urging me on. It was getting late. Enough chitchat.

"Y'all wouldn't happen to have your suits with you, would you?"

"Of course," Thad chuckled. "Never go anywhere without them."

I cleared my throat. "Great. So, here's the thing...."

The next ten minutes passed by like molasses. It was already seven-thirty, and we hadn't even started dismantling the six remaining spikes. But this was it. Tonight was our last chance to climb the tree before the final piece of scaffolding was rolled away and the celebrity musicians arrived for soundcheck for tomorrow's performances.

We had no choice but to wait.

One video call later from my parents — and after Rodney's two attempts to leave in search of a hot pretzel — things finally started moving. I noticed before anyone. Thad rounded the corner of the Comcast Building first, followed by a dozen or so cosplayers. It was weird not seeing them in costume; instead, they were all bundled up in winter coats, hats, and scarves.

They passed by the colorful window display at FAO Schwarz toy store, and then one by one, they lined up directly across from us in front of the Comcast Building. Like they were preparing for a game of Red Rover. Thad and I made eye contact and nodded. I wasn't sure how this was going to work, but I trusted him. Maybe because he sort of owed me one.

Whatever the reason, we had no choice. The Mortal Kombat League of the Lower East Side — no matter how "unique" — was our only hope.

For a moment, nothing special happened. People roamed around with shopping bags, snapped pictures of the tree, and carried on as usual. Thad's crew stood in formation with their hands behind their backs, but no one paid them any mind until —

"Hit it, Melanie!" Thad yelled.

The girl named Melanie broke her stance to press play on a portable speaker resting on the ground. She quickly returned to her post, and as the beat of the music grew louder, she hollered, "And five, six, seven, eight!"

In unison, the cosplayers ripped off their coats, revealing their over-the-top costumes underneath. Hats and scarves were tossed aside, replaced with green Hammer pants, gold belts, spiky headbands and shoulder pads, and everything in between. Thad and his friends were more than a bunch of Mortal Kombat ninjas and warriors. Suddenly they were robots, their arms popping and locking to the music in perfect harmony.

Their performance was better than we could've hoped for. Honestly, I thought they'd show up in costume and start kicking and slapping each other. Maybe throw some of those green fireballs around the place to shake things up. But this? Crumping to "Bad Romance" like a bunch of Lady Gaga backup dancers? This was unexpected.

But very much appreciated.

"This is it," I said as people took notice and started gathering around the dancers. "Now's our chance."

Rodney pumped the air. "Go go go!"

Clue and I raced toward the tree, keeping an eye out for any stragglers who may be watching us instead of the flash mob. Clue climbed up first. As I waited for my turn, I studied the group dancing. I couldn't believe it. *Who knew?* I thought. Who knew all that talent was hiding under those dorky costumes?

A shower of snow sprinkled down on my face as Clue's legs disappeared through the branches. I followed up after her.

And then we got to work.

CHAPTER 55

By now we were a couple of pros. Sort of. At least climbing a sixty-nine-foot tree, even with the snow, didn't seem as impossible as it had the first go around — except for the wind. And the sway. Those two things still very much made me wish for an extra ten milligrams of Lexapro. Anything to quell the anxiety throbbing in my chest every time an icy breeze ripped through the topmost branches.

I felt like King Kong teetering on top of the Empire State Building. Just one wrong move away from splattering onto the pavement below.

"I think you're getting the hang of this," Clue said ironically, looking back as we climbed. There was a softer edge to her voice. She actually sounded like a friend, a partner in crime (literally), rather than a drill sergeant barking orders.

"Thanks," I said. "I've been practicing."

Although it was freezing outside, a layer of sweat clung to my back by the time we reached the tree's peak, safely hidden beneath the marshmallow dome. I hoisted myself onto one side of the platform to catch my breath. Meanwhile, Clue was on the other side, goggles secured and already whipping out her blowtorch. The dome came to life the moment she released the blue flame. Half the star was missing, but it didn't matter. Thousands of mirror-ball reflections bounced off the crystals still intact, covering the inside of the dome in what appeared to be our own personal galaxy of stars.

"Hey," said Clue, suddenly removing her goggles so they could rest on her forehead. She kept the torch burning, and I couldn't help but stare at the crystals' reflection dancing across her tan skin. "Thank you for what you did down there. This whole operation would've been blown if it weren't for your quick thinking." Her voice remained soft and low as she carefully chose each word. Like a poet crafting every line, stanza, and syllable with extreme care. "I'm glad you're here."

Words I never thought I'd hear Clue say.

Words that, in some powerful way, made me want to lean in closer.

"Me too."

We slipped into our usual rhythm like a well-oiled machine, as if this were nothing more than a nine-to-five we'd been grinding away at for years. Clue cut the spike, I lowered the spike, and Rodney dumped the spike into a backpack.

Mom was always a fan of assembly lines like this. She believed they got a job done "lickety-split," so it wasn't much of a surprise when she organized one to help Aunt Celeste unpack her apartment. Basically, Dad would pull out one of Aunt Celeste's gaudy trinkets from a cardboard box and pass it to me. I'd carry it to Mom. Mom would march it over to Aunt Celeste. And Aunt Celeste would scurry around her 700-hundred-square-foot sardine can until she found the perfect spot for said trinket.

Mom would be proud of us for using her assembly line method — if only it wasn't to steal a giant Christmas tree topper worth hundreds of thousands of dollars.

I'd resigned myself to the fact that the shimmering sparks spitting from Clue's torch as she sliced away were just part of the job. A crazy, unethical, un*lawful* job…but yeah. Plus, the branches were wet with snow, which would definitely snuff out any potential fires this time.

At least that's what I told myself.

Clue was over halfway through cutting the last spike — *so close* — when Rodney's voice crackled over the din of the city below. I reached my radio first.

"What's up, Rodney?"

"Weeee may have a problem."

Quick as a reflex, Clue slid her goggles up as we anxiously waited for more.

"This little girl — five? Possibly six? She just pointed my way," Rodney whispered. "I think she's seen me. But, I mean, she's such a cute little thing, so I really don't think it's anything to worry about. She's got these little kitten ears on her beanie, and her coat is this incredibly bright shade of —"

"RODNEY."

Clue hissed right along with me, even though I was the one holding the radio. "What's going on, dude?" I urged. "What's happening?"

A brief pause. And then —

"Uh oh."

"WHAT?"

"She's walking this way," said Rodney. "Toward the trunk." His voice accelerated into a completely new octave. "And she's bringing her mum!"

"You've *got* to be kidding me," said Clue to no one in particular. She yanked down her goggles and resumed working, leaving me to think on my feet. Which, again, were currently almost seventy feet off the ground.

I wrenched out my phone again and called Thad. From what I could see, most of the League members had stuck around Rockefeller Center. A few were ice skating, but we didn't need everyone. Just enough warriors and creatures to make a scene. I quickly begged him for one last favor, and within seconds, the place was filled with an encore performance.

More music. More dancing. More insane costumes.

"Okay!" said Rodney after what felt like the longest fifteen seconds of our lives. "Cat girl and mummy have stopped. They're checking out the dancers!"

"We need to move," said Clue. *"Now."*

She killed the torch as I collected the last glistening spike and dumped it into the canvas bag. The star was completely wrecked. Instead of a twelve-pointed showcase of Christmas spirit, it was now little more than an oversized disco ball. For a moment, I wondered what the workers would say when they pulled back the white dome tomorrow night. I wondered what Clue's *dad* would say.

But that was a terrifying thought, so I quickly pushed it aside.

"All yours, Rodney!" I relayed into the radio, giving the rope a good tug.

Before Clue and I threw all caution to the wind, slid off the tiny platform, and hurled ourselves down the tree.

CHAPTER 56

It was a bummer not thanking Thad and the other cosplayers in person — not that we had much of a choice. As soon as our feet hit the ground, Clue and I each slung a backpack over our shoulders, and the three of us started speed walking away from the tree as discreetly as possible. Thad's crew continued breaking it down to some weird techno music.

"Blimey, that was close," Rodney panted as he readjusted the straps of his own backpack. "I thought we were done for!"

Unfortunately, he may have spoken too soon.

Just as we were stepping off the curb to cross 49th Street, Rodney's backpack split wide open, and all you could hear was the metallic clang of two fifteen-pound spikes toppling onto the pavement.

"What happened?" shrieked Clue.

We raced back to help scoop up the goods — but a moment too late. A stout cop with a surprising resemblance to Paul Blart saw the whole thing unfold, which undoubtedly raised several enormous red flags.

"Hey!" he hollered, throwing up a hand. "Kids! Wait right there."

"I don't know," said Rodney. "One of the spikes must've torn a seam or something."

It didn't matter. Whatever had happened, happened, and we were now a trio of sitting ducks with a stolen fortune on our backs.

"You think you can carry it by hand?" asked Clue. "If you pinch the seams together right here?"

She didn't wait for a response. She was already jogging — or, as fast as you can move with thirty extra pounds on your back — toward a yellow taxi, her own spikes jangling dangerously with every step. Rodney and I followed.

"Excuse me, sir?" Clue said hastily. She knocked on the rear passenger window about a hundred times in the span of three seconds; the glass lowered as the taxi driver turned in his seat to face us. "Do you know there's dog poop in your backseat?"

My neck snapped the same time as Rodney's. Our eyes locked, and judging from the size of his pupils, I'm guessing he was just as shocked. *What was she doing?*

"No poo," said the driver, his dark beard quivering with the shake of his head. "No dogs allowed, see?" He tapped a small, laminated sign on the back of the passenger seat headrest. "So no. No poo."

"Well," said Clue, "either you've got some serious dookie back here...or that is one nasty, melted Snickers."

The driver craned his neck, trying his best to see. Clue stole another glance at the cop wobbling down the sidewalk toward us.

"Trust me, sir. This mess is huge. I'm thinking Saint Bernard...possibly Great Dane? It's hard to say, really." She nudged me in the arm and pointed back into the taxi. "Or do you think horse?"

"Horse?!"

That did it.

The taxi driver began muttering angrily in his native tongue. He tore off his seatbelt, flung open the door, and scurried over to our side of the car.

But Clue was much faster. She tossed her backpack through the open window, and before I had a chance to object, she wrenched mine from my shoulders and did the same. "Come on!" she said, grabbing my wrist and pulling me around to the other side of the taxi. "Rodney, get in!" Which he did in a flash, racing behind us and climbing into the backseat.

"Hey!" The driver peered over the roof of the taxi. "Hey, what you do!"

"Kids!" Blart was now crossing the street. "I'm ordering you to *stop!*"

By the time I looked back at the taxi, Clue was crawling across the center console, the soles of her boots flailing in the air.

"What are you —?"

"Come on!" she said, flopping into the passenger seat. "Hurry!"

The taxi driver was racing around the trunk of his car, and the cop was only steps away. There was no time. No time to apologize or think through a list of possible options.

So I jumped in. Locked the doors.

And hit the gas.

CHAPTER 57

Tires screeched as the cab lurched forward, drowning out the screams behind us.

"Step on it," said Clue. She leaned toward the dash; her head swiveled left to right as she scoped out the area.

"What are we doing?" I asked, squeezing the steering wheel until my arms ached. "This is crazy!"

"Just drive."

As we reached the next intersection, though, the light turned red, and I had to slam on the brakes. "Why aren't one of you driving? Y'all know the city better than I do. There's only one stoplight in Shady Springs, and the max speed is, like, 35."

My fingers tapped the wheel as the pedestrian signal slowly counted down. I wasn't a fan of car theft, but I also didn't like the idea of waiting around for law enforcement to catch up.

Clue shrugged. "Neither of us has our license."

The wires in my brain crackled before ultimately blowing a fuse. I'm sure the look on my face showed it. "You literally stole the Rockefeller Center Christmas Tree star, and *now* you're worried about legalities?"

"We've got trouble, people!" Rodney's voice cut in. From the rearview mirror, I could see him peeking out the back window. "Copper's coming this way!"

I glanced in the side mirror, and my heart dunked into the pit of my stomach. He was right. The cop car was still a good distance away, but there was no denying the flashing red and blue lights were meant for us.

Green.

Finally, the light changed — but I couldn't move.

"Nate, go!" said Clue.

"I can't! People are still walking across!"

"It doesn't matter because you've got the—"

"This is New York, mate!" Rodney boomed. "MOW THEM DOWN!"

It was as if his voice dumped a cement block on my foot. The pedal hit the floorboard, and we were off, zooming up Sixth Avenue at what felt like the speed of light.

"Where are we going?" I asked, doing my best to weave through the swarm of cars.

"Central Park," said Clue. "We can lose them in there."

Several minutes later — at Clue's subtle command to *"Stop the car!"* — I yanked the taxi against a curb just outside the Ritz-Carlton hotel and threw the gearshift into park. We all jumped out, grabbed a backpack, and proceeded to engage in some serious jaywalking as we ran across the busy street.

"This way!" said Clue, barely dodging a horse-drawn carriage exiting the park.

I stole one more look at the glowing lights of Sixth Avenue. Paul Blart rounded the corner, the same corner we'd just left, but his screaming cruiser whipped right past our stolen taxi. The tightness in my chest relaxed ever so slightly.

"Nate..." Clue's warm hand squeezed my own, and I found myself staring down at our entwined fingers. "We have to go...."

I nodded, before stepping into the shadows and letting the trees of Central Park swallow me whole.

CHAPTER 58

"You were out awful late last night."

Aunt Celeste's sky-blue eyes winked at me above the rim of her porcelain teacup as she savored another sip. She was fishing for information, but there was no bite or disappointment in her voice. Actually, she almost sounded amused, and the twinkle in her eyes offered a glimpse into all the stupid scenarios she was concocting in her head. Like maybe I'd been out kissing girls all night. Or partying with rockstars.

We were seated at the tiny bistro table in her tiny kitchen. I downed my coffee while she fed Gerdy a piece of buttered toast.

"Do anything exciting?" she continued, wriggling her eyebrows.

Sure did. Let's see.... After climbing the Rockefeller Center Christmas Tree for the third time, I helped steal a taxi, broke the speed limit enough to be charged with reckless driving, AND hid some more pieces of a crazy-expensive tree topper, which I also helped steal. Oh, and I think I might have a crush on the girl who practically threatened to kill us the other day. So, yeah, really exciting stuff!

I carried my coffee mug over to the sink. Knowing I *couldn't* say those things — no matter how cool Aunt Celeste may be — I stuck with the usual, "It was okay. Just hung out with those kids I met at the ice rink again."

After tossing Gerdy the remaining crust, Aunt Celeste rinsed out her teacup and gathered up her rehearsal bag and giant purse. "Okay, then," she said, beaming as if she were about to embark on a seven-day cruise. "I'm off to rehearsal! Tomorrow's the big day, remember, so I'm sure the director will want an extra-thorough practice." She lingered at the open front door. "You'll be okay for dinner?"

I nodded. "Absolutely."

If she only knew, I thought. *Dinner's the* last *thing on my mind tonight.*

"Break a leg!"

Aunt Celeste squealed, overjoyed with my use of theater lingo, patted her hive of blue hair, and rushed out the door.

I was stupid to think today would be different. I thought, maybe, I could relax, seeing as all the stealing was behind us now. No more gearing up in all-black. No more sneaking around. No more scaling seven-story Christmas trees. Nothing to stress over, right? But halfway through another *Full House* rerun with Gerdy, it hit me.

Tonight was *the* night. The big reveal.

The night everything changed.

Millions of people all around the country would be tuning in to their televisions. They'd see what we'd done...and it would only be a matter of time before we were caught.

Stop, Nate, I told myself. *You're fine. Clue's plan is solid. You're all fine.*

Despite the pep talk, I turned off the TV and spread out on the couch, choosing a few extra hours of sleep over an afternoon of worry.

Boom boom boom.

My eyes flitted open, burning as they adjusted to the window's light. I blinked, and slowly the room swam into focus. Gerdy was passed out under the coffee table. I must've been exhausted because my head was throbbing, which usually meant I'd slept too hard. But something else was pounding....

Boom boom boom.

The door.

After finally registering the noise, I crawled from the couch and shuffled across the living room carpet, yawning — until I saw her.

"Clue?" I was suddenly wide awake, my vision crystal-clear. "What are you doing here? What time is it?"

"Almost four," she said, stepping inside without waiting for an invitation. "I rushed over right after school." She almost sounded out of breath, like she'd literally jogged the last few blocks. Like she couldn't get here fast enough.

"What's up?" I asked, a little hesitantly.

She stared at me for what seemed like forever, letting a deep breath roll out of her, and I started to wonder if she was making me wait on purpose. Forcing me to suffer. More than anything, I wanted to know what was going through her mind, but I had no idea.

Finally, as if she decided I'd sweated long enough, she dove into her backpack to retrieve something.

"This," she said, holding it up like a piece of evidence in court.

My notebook. For whatever reason, Clue had my notebook.

And she looked horrified.

CHAPTER 59

"How did you...?"

I closed the door and followed Clue into the living room. Gerdy, now awake, bleated anxiously at our guest, but I shooed her away so we could sit on the couch.

"How did you get that?"

"You left it yesterday," said Clue. "On the coffee table."

I wasn't even aware my notebook had been missing, but now that I saw it in her hand, a queasiness churned in my stomach. *Please tell me you didn't open it. Please tell me you didn't read anything.*

That's just the kind of writer I was. I didn't show my work to anyone, not even family. Plus — I swallowed at the thought — I'd hate for her to see...

"You wrote about me," she said, as if reading my mind. Her eyes flicked to her lap, and when she looked up again, I wondered if she was blushing a little. But soon enough her face hardened into stone again. "Why?"

If the couch cushion would've slipped open like a trap door at that exact moment, I'd have been eternally grateful.

"I'm a writer, Clue," I said, shrugging. As if that explained it. "I...like writing about the things around me. Things that inspire me."

"The sunrise. Rodents. I get that."

Ouch. I cringed at the idea of her reading about the rabid rat in a heap of hot garbage.

"But you also wrote about me," she said, her voice quieter.

She opened the notebook then and began reading, as if trying to prove her point, as if trying to remind me. But I knew those words all too well.

"Peeking around the branches," she read, "her face met me like an unforeseen angel, and I was somehow stunned to find she looked even more beautiful in the hazy glow of the Christmas tree lights. How was that possible? How had I never noticed the splash of freckles, as if someone had sprinkled a dusting of cinnamon across her button nose."

Heat rushed to my face. "Clue, I —"

She ignored and kept reading.

"But outward beauty isn't everything, of course. What makes this girl truly special is the bond she shares with her mother. You can hear it in their laughter as they place the ornaments together. You can see it through the girl's actions as she meets her mother's every need, like a child mending a fallen bird's broken wing...."

Her voice trailed off, and when she dared to look up again, her eyes were red and puffy. "Is that why you stuck around?" she breathed. "To watch us? So we could feed your imagination?"

"You guys approached *me*, remember?" I said, suddenly feeling cornered. "I'm only here because I was jumped in the middle of an ice rink. You found *me*."

Clue tossed the notebook aside and gave her face one quick wipe with her coat sleeve. "Well, I didn't think you'd be writing our biography."

It was as if I'd been sucking on cotton in my sleep. "I just...I just wanted to capture those moments," I choked out. "They were beautiful. You're —"

I caught myself and swallowed.

Don't dig this ditch any deeper, Nate. Don't go there.

But it was too late. The tears welling up in Clue's eyes told me I'd said more than enough.

"Nate..." Her voice was thin, with no backbone left. She stared at me with glassy eyes, slowly shaking her head.

It seemed I was at the very bottom of that ditch. In fact, boxing Goro again sounded better than having this conversation. But deep down, I also knew I *wanted* to have it. I'd chickened out on McKenna, and she ended up moving on. Maybe that was meant to be.

But this felt different. *Clue* felt different.

"I'm sorry if my words made you uncomfortable," I said, finally. And then, thanks to some invisible nudge, I added, "But I'm not sorry I wrote them. I meant every single one."

She stood and headed for the door.

"Clue, what's really going on? What's this all about?"

"Why did you write those things?" she asked again, spinning around and practically glaring at me. "Do you...do you have feelings for me?"

My brain moved faster than my mouth, tumbling over everything I wanted to say. Everything I was thinking. I'd known Clue less than a week. Did she feel the same way? If I told her, would she laugh? Would she slap me?

She doesn't feel the same way, I convinced myself. *She can't. If she did, she wouldn't be so upset.*

I started to speak, but Clue's palm was in my face before I could get out a single word.

"You know what, don't answer that."

"Clue." I grabbed her hand as she lowered it and took a brave step closer.

But unlike yesterday, she pulled away this time. "Please stop," she whispered. "I can't think about this. I" — She started backing away — "I've got to get home to Mom."

Something between us broke. Changed. Clue was like the tide, retreating into the sea, pulling away from me again. I wanted to hold on tighter.

But, of course, the ocean is unstoppable.

"This is why I don't like getting close to people."

Her words felt too raw, too honest, too open. Part of me wondered if she meant to keep them to herself, safe inside her mind. Clue's hand was on the doorknob, and she might as well have been talking to the wall because her voice barely carried. But when she turned, one last time, I knew she wanted me to hear.

"Knowing all of this — knowing you feel this way..." She shook her head, and I could see a shimmer of tears running down her cheeks. "It just makes it harder when you leave."

And then she was gone.

CHAPTER 60

Pancakes. More specifically, *chocolate chip pancakes*.

That's what Rodney was craving, so instead of watching NBC's tree lighting special at his place like we'd originally planned, we met up at some all-night diner on Sixth Avenue. I ordered a spicy breakfast burrito, and Clue stuck with eggs and toast. We tucked ourselves away in a corner booth, putting us in perfect view of one of the many TVs mounted along the walls.

"Well, C," said Rodney, still a little stuffy, "this time tomorrow you'll be New York City's Christmas hero." He hovered over his short stack with his camera, twisting the plate until the cloud of whipped cream and rivers of syrup were perfectly positioned. "What time are you thinking about heading to the park?" He snapped a couple of photos. "Right after school?"

That had been the plan since day one. Clue would "stumble" onto the stash of spikes during an afternoon stroll. She'd report it to the police. And she'd be remembered as the girl who saved Christmas.

Luckily, the NYPD wouldn't know that Clue Perez **a)** wasn't prone to stumbling and **b)** would never, ever waste time on a casual afternoon stroll through Central Park just for fun.

"I don't know," Clue shrugged, stirring her scrambled eggs in a mound of ketchup.

It was the most she'd said all evening, and I knew why. I knew she was still ticked at me for writing about her, still upset with me for sharing my feelings.

It just makes it harder when you leave.

She was right. Even with the cold shoulder, even with the silent treatment, I hated to think about leaving her and Rodney on Friday.

It just makes it harder when you leave.

When you leave.

There was something deeper there, I just knew it. It was the way she'd said it. The way she'd looked at me when she'd said it. Her dad jetted off in the blink of an eye…and now she was slowly losing her mom too.

Clue was all too familiar with the people in her life leaving.

People she cared about.

A little while later, just as I was adding sugar to my second cup of coffee, Kelly Clarkson began wrapping up her final performance at Rockefeller Center. A flaming-red coat swallowed her from head to toe, and the high def did an excellent job at showing the vapors escaping into the chilly air as she belted away. Despite the cold, though, she sang every note perfectly.

When she finished, the camera cut away to the hosts, who looked like they were about to freeze their faces off. I wondered if they were really smiling or just grimacing through the pain.

"Absolutely beautiful," said the woman, her gloved hands gripping the microphone. The crowds clapped and cheered behind her. "Thank you to Kelly and all the other artists joining us tonight for a *very* special occasion. As you may or may not know, it's been twenty-one years since the Rockefeller Center Christmas Tree received a new star, but I am pleased to announce that we are just moments away from revealing a brand-new star designed by one of Brooklyn's very own."

More clapping.

"However, before we unveil this masterpiece, it is my privilege to introduce you to the incredibly talented designer himself — Mr. Emelio Perez!"

The TV erupted with applause as Clue's dad sprinted on stage with his own microphone. The same man I'd seen mentioned in all those articles online.

"Thank you, thank you," he said, holding out a hand. He wore a black suit underneath a long wool coat, and his dark slicked-back hair refused to move, despite the wind.

I shifted uncomfortably in the sticky vinyl booth. Rodney and I stole glances at Clue, but she remained focused, arms crossed, eyes zeroed in on the television screen.

Mr. Perez nodded until the noise died down. "I must say that when I started fixing automobiles and playing around with car parts at the start of my career, I never imagined it would lead me here." That earned some more cheers. "I always loved creating things," said Mr. Perez, "even as a boy growing up in Peru." His voice grew thick with emotion, but he pressed on. "My parents sacrificed everything by coming here to the States. They wanted a better life for us. They wanted to give me the opportunity to dream. Well," he said, "many dreams have come true for me over the past few years, but I must say tonight outshines them all. Thank you to the beautiful city of New York for trusting me with such a special task. And thanks to each of you for coming out tonight. This star now belongs to all of you!" More cheering. "Enjoy!"

The crowds on TV went wild; even some of the customers in the diner cheered or beat the table with their palms.

Not Clue.

She stayed glued to the screen with complete concentration, like if she blinked she'd unravel everything she was silently processing. But she didn't look angry, even after seeing her dad parade around on stage. She seemed almost sad.

I wondered if it was because Mr. Perez — in the midst of his whole "dreams coming true" spiel — didn't mention her or her mom. Not once.

CHAPTER 61

It was the second host's turn to speak. His chunky glasses magnified his eyes to almost alien status, and if Rudolph could've seen this man's nose, he'd have been jealous of its bright shade of red.

Still, Mr. Reporter Guy smiled through the cold.

"Ladies and gentlemen," he said, "you've heard the songs; you've seen the talent. But now, the moment we've all been waiting for has finally arrived. I'm told we are just thirty seconds away from lighting the tree here at Rockefeller Center and unveiling its new star. Are you ready?"

He turned to encourage the onlookers, and they responded with a resounding *Yes!*

"Okay," he said, facing the camera again. "Let's count it down."

Suddenly, the mood shifted. A band of drums beat rapidly, and the lights dimmed around the entire plaza. I thought I was going to puke. After a few agonizing moments, the hosts began leading every TV viewer, every online streamer, and every person around the ice rink in a ten-second countdown.

"Ten! Nine! Eight! Seven!"

I tried to play it cool like Clue and Rodney. I tried to sit there, watch the screen, and pretend like this was the most exciting thing I'd ever witnessed.

But that spicy breakfast burrito was bubbling away.

"Six! Five! Four!"

Even the cooks had come out to count down, their spatulas in the air.

"Three!

I tried to ground myself by bouncing my legs beneath the table.

"Two!"

Anything to keep me from running out the door.

"ONE!"

Thousands of colorful lights sprang to life, morphing the tree into a towering beacon of Christmas cheer. The cables holding the tree topper cover in place were pulled…the marshmallow dome lifted…and the whole thing fell away in a dramatic swish.

The camera cut to the hosts, but they were too busy gaping in disbelief. The drums crashed to a halt. And all of Rockefeller Center sucked in a collective, gasping breath.

The star — much to everyone's horror — was gone.

CHAPTER 62

After what felt like an eternity, the female host suddenly seemed to remember they were on live television and acknowledged the camera again.

"I don't believe it," she fumbled, holding a hand to her earpiece. "From what I'm hearing and from what we just witnessed…the new Rockefeller Center Christmas Tree star" — She shook her head — "seems to have *vanished*."

Behind her, confused whispering grew into disgruntled chaos — and the diner was no different.

"Look!" said one of the cooks, pointing. "The star's gone!"

Some motorcycle dude slid off his barstool. "What's going on?" he demanded, folding his arms across his leather jacket and peering up at the TV, waiting for an explanation.

"Is this a joke?"

"How does a thing like that go missing?"

"Do you think it's for real?"

Our booth was the only corner in the place not asking questions. I glanced over at Clue. She still hadn't taken her eyes off the broadcast, but although everything she'd wanted, everything she'd hoped for, was playing out in front of her, there was no hint of a smile or any sort of satisfaction in her face.

Does she regret it?

I almost leaned across the table and congratulated her, just to see what she'd say —

"Okay, it appears we may have some breaking news surrounding tonight's bizarre events."

My attention snapped back to the TV. A hush fell over the diner as everyone waited for the female host to continue. The camera zoomed out just enough to catch the newcomers standing next to her, and as soon as I saw them, my stomach dropped to the gummy tile floor. The reporters were now talking to a police officer and a taxi driver.

The same taxi driver whose cab we stole.

Rodney and I exchanged looks, and even Clue's eyes shifted uncomfortably for once.

"This is Phillip Hadid," said the hostess, addressing the camera. "A cab driver here in New York who has served our city for nearly thirty years. Mr. Hadid was in the audience tonight enjoying the tree lighting ceremony with his family, but after the star appeared to be missing just minutes ago, he found the nearest officer he could." She motioned to the policeman, and he silently nodded in return.

"Now, Mr. Hadid," the male host chimed in, "you were telling us about a strange encounter you had just last night not too far from here. Around 49th and Sixth. Can you walk us through what happened?"

Mr. Hadid stepped closer to the outstretched microphone. "Yes, of course," he said with that thick accent I remembered all too well. "I was taking break, and some kids came and knock on my window. Say there was, uh, waste. In backseat."

"Waste?" asked the host.

"Yes. Uh...poop. Dog poops."

"And what time was this?"

Mr. Hadid thought for a second. "Around 10 o'clock, I think."

"And what happened next?"

"So I get out and tell them no. No poops." He flung his arms out, like an umpire calling safe. "I walk around to other side of car, and they jump in and *steal* car!"

The reporter nodded. "And you said you saw something unusual?"

"Yes. Sticking out of one of their bags. Some kind of spikes. Expensive-looking."

Clue and I redirected our attention to Rodney, who was already sliding down in the seat, covering his eyes as he sank farther and farther.

"Expensive-looking spikes?"

"Yes," said Mr. Hadid. "Like" — He motioned with his hands, desperately trying to convey his message — "silver, glittery spikes. Huge things. Like they would belong to a star, I don't know."

"Officer Lewinski," the hostess continued, "what do *you* make of this?"

The policeman cleared his throat. "We do feel this is worth looking into. Could it be a coincidence and a completely isolated incident, sure." He shrugged. "But maybe not."

"Before we say goodbye, Mr. Hadid, is there anything you can tell us about these teens? Anything you remember about them at all?"

No.

No no no no no.

All four walls seemed to suddenly squeeze in around us. I wanted to rip off my coat, it was so stifling hot. I wanted to rewind the broadcast, go back in time just a couple of minutes, and chuck the TVs out into the street.

The taxi driver nodded. "Three of them," he said. "Two boys and a girl." He thought for a moment more. "The girl was pretty short, darker skin. One of the boys have glasses. The other" — He drew his hands up to his scalp — "fluffy, curly hair. Blonde, I think."

And that was it.

Game over.

CHAPTER 63

The news station might as well have thrown up a poster with our faces on it, because about two seconds after Mr. Hadid shared his descriptions, all eyes were on us. People turned around in their booths. A couple of kids pointed, only to have their parents whisper something in their ears and push their fingers down.

The news just described the Three Stooges. And there we were, in the flesh.

"I think we should go," mumbled Clue, her lips barely moving but her eyes dancing around the diner. "Right now."

It was strange to hear her speak unprompted for the first time in hours. I could tell Rodney was just as surprised, but we had bigger fish to fry. We had to get out of there.

"Come on," said Clue.

We slid out of our booth and calmly — but quickly — headed for the door, doing our best to ignore everyone's stares. An old woman narrowed her eyes suspiciously as we passed and practically poked me in the ribs with her cane. I nodded politely and kept moving.

A gust of icy wind pummeled us the moment we stepped outside, and I'd never been more thankful. I gulped down the fresh air.

WOOP! WOOP!

Before any of us could say a word, blue lights were flashing everywhere. Two cruisers barreled onto the sidewalk, forming a sort of triangle with the front of the diner. Trapping us. Doors burst open, and three cops came running out, shouting "Put your hands up! Put your hands up!" as they moved in.

We did as we were told.

"Thanks a lot!" yelled Clue.

She was looking back at the diner, where everyone — including the cooks, waitresses, and even cranky ol' granny — was pressed against the glass walls, taking in the show. Someone had obviously snitched.

"I hope you all choke on your pancakes!"

Typical Clue. Going down swinging.

A few feet away, Rodney's fate unfolded exactly as I'd feared. He was escorted to his own car, and even as the cop ducked Rodney's head inside, I could still hear him muttering some random rap. Probably to keep from crying.

"I said these chains may try to hold us, but I promise I won't make a fuss." Rodney jangled his handcuffs. "Be brave. Be strong," he moaned. "Just know we did no wrong."

But we did.

We did do something wrong.

We stole.

Thanks to Dad's obsession, I'd watched my fair share of true crime, which made this whole thing even more surreal. As Clue and I were cuffed and led to the second car, I suddenly felt like I was starring in a special holiday episode of *America's Most Wanted*.

Because I was a criminal.

I was a thief.

CHAPTER 64

Clue said nothing the entire ride to the police station. Every once in a while I'd sneak a look her way, torn between asking if she was okay or saying something at least halfway encouraging, but I always let it go. She seemed content just staring at the lights blurring past the window.

I hated this — and not just the fact that I was being *arrested*. I hated this new canyon that separated Clue and me. We'd made so much progress over the past few days…and now it was all ruined. We were right back to where we started, maybe even worse.

One step forward. A hundred steps back.

We reached the station, and before we could even blink, officers were pushing us through a pair of glass doors. As they unlocked our cuffs, the writer in me couldn't help but take in the place. It was as dull as you could imagine. Gray walls and gray desks and gray floors, all illuminated by blinding fluorescent lights that buzzed and flickered sporadically. In fact, the lobby was so depressing that I started to miss Aunt Celeste's pink Christmas tree and Gerdy's crazy assortment of toys strewn everywhere.

Aunt Celeste.

What would she say?

Probably not much. Nothing compared to the wrath that Mom and Dad would unleash when they found out their felon of a son was doing time in the slammer.

"Arms up," said one of the cops after we'd removed our beanies and coats.

We stood there, arms and legs splayed like three stupid starfish, while officers patted us down.

"You mates enjoying your evening?" Rodney chuckled nervously.

The officers kept frisking. One confiscated Rodney's camera. "We were," he sighed. "Then you three happened."

Once cleared, they herded us back to a holding cell. I tried not to glance at the other detainees, but it wasn't easy. An old man was muttering to himself in the corner of his cell, and another guy was knocking against the metal bars of his with dirty knuckles. His wide, bloodshot eyes followed us without blinking.

I swallowed and kept moving.

Inmates. These are my fellow INMATES.

I'm one of them.

The thought didn't seem real — *couldn't* be real — even as Officer Daniels stepped aside and ushered us into our own cell. Even as he slid the bars shut with a jarring CLANG.

Even as he locked the door and stepped away.

"You'll get your phone calls in just a few," he barked, before disappearing down the hall.

Without making a peep, Clue headed to the back of the cell and plopped down on the bed's thin mattress. Rodney let his back slide down the cement wall until he was seated on the floor.

"I can't believe this," I muttered to no one in particular. Probably just to my deeply damaged conscience.

This wasn't supposed to happen. We're not supposed to be here. How do we get out?!

"Better believe it, sonny."

A scraggly voice tore into my spiral. I peered through the bars, across the hall, and there was our neighbor, Mr. Crazy Eyes, grinning a toothless grin.

"Whatcha in for?" he jeered, licking his red gums. "Drugs? You kill somebody?" He pressed his face eagerly between two bars. "Somebody try to kill *you*?"

I could feel him staring at the faint purple bruise under my eye. My battle wound.

The man started cackling. I staggered away from the cell bars and quickly slid to the floor beside Rodney, doing my best to angle away from the hyena next door.

"We've got to get out of here," I whispered. "This is crazy."

"Great idea," said Clue.

Rodney and I jerked our attention her way, but she kept her head lowered, elbows resting on her knees as she stared at the concrete between her boots.

"When you figure that one out, let me know."

"Clue?" said Rodney. "You alright there?"

She finally looked up, the gaze in her eyes hard as steel. "I was just thinking Nate could write us out of here. Ask for some pen and paper. Put the officers in a story." She shrugged. "Maybe they'll be so honored that they'll let us go."

Her words, her eyes were meant for me and me alone. That much was obvious. Rodney might as well not have been in the room. But I didn't get it. Couldn't she see that everything I wrote about her was good? Didn't she understand that?

A mountain out of a molehill.

Something my mom said often.

After a few painful moments of silence, Rodney stood. "Awkwardddd," he observed, dusting off his pants.

Still nothing — either from Clue or me. She'd dropped her head again, and the storm of thoughts spinning inside me made it difficult to pull out words and string them together.

Rodney must've noticed. Either that or his bowels just had really good timing.

"Officer?" he said, approaching the cell door. "Excuse me?" He waited a few seconds, ignoring Mr. Crazy Eyes, but when no one came, he started knocking on the bars. "Oi! Anyone there?" More knocking. Louder knocking. "Helloooo—"

"Easy, buddy."

Officer Daniels appeared in the hallway, his keys jangling with every step. He popped the last bite of some sort of pastry in his mouth before approaching our cell.

"Is there a problem?" he mumbled, mouth full.

"I need to use the loo."

Officer Daniels licked a drop of leftover icing from his thumb and nodded, gesturing to the steel toilet in the corner of our cell. "Well, there you go."

Rodney leaned closer. "But, sir," he whispered, "there's a *lady* in here."

From the dull look on his face, it was obvious Officer Daniels didn't care if there was a *giraffe* in the room, much less a lady. Still, after an eyeroll and a few grunts while fumbling through his keys, he unlocked the door and led Rodney down the hall to the actual restroom.

CHAPTER 65

Slumped against the wall, I stared at my damp Converses. Whatever slush they'd accumulated trudging through the city was now melted out on the concrete floor. I stared at my wrists. They were free as a bird now, but I could still feel the cold metal latched around them. Could still remember the cuffs pressing into my bones.

Clue was just as quiet as ever, and it was torture. In the stillness, I swore I could smell her perfume, that cozy vanilla scent sneaking its way to my corner and making my stomach flip in the best way. I wanted to sit next to her. I wanted to breathe her in, look into those beautiful brown eyes of hers, and say whatever it was that would fix us.

I wanted us to be okay.

Do something, Nate.

I reached into my jeans pocket and felt the folded letter, still there. The frisking earlier hadn't been very thorough. My words were the last thing Clue wanted to read, but you leave a confused writer home alone all day with questions about the girl he hurt — the girl he may or may not be falling for — and a bit of word vomiting is bound to happen.

I know my words aren't your favorite thing, I had written. *But they're all I've got. I'm a writer. Taking away my words is like taking a fish's water.*

She could ball it up, throw it way, or shred the whole thing into a million pieces. Whatever happened, at least I could say I tried. Because it was the *not* trying that scared me. The not knowing what could've been.

But just as I got to my feet, just as I worked up enough courage to hand Clue the letter —

BOOM BOOM BOOM.

"Let's hurry it up in there, Mr. Donoghue." It was Officer Daniels, beating on the restroom door, ordering Rodney out. "This is jail, not a day spa."

Before I could hand Clue the letter and explain, Rodney was back in our cage.

"Phew," he said, shaking the curls from his eyes. "I feel *loads* better."

Eventually we were each allowed our one phone call. When Officer Daniels returned to escort one of us to the phone room, though, Clue suddenly piped up and insisted on going first.

"Don't worry," she mumbled, barely looking our way as she stepped out into the hall. "I'll handle it."

"Handle it," mocked Rodney once she was gone. "What's that supposed to mean? She's met my mum. The only handling of this will be my butt in my room, no camera, and no dating until I'm married."

"Sounds about right," I agreed, plopping down on the bed. "I just hope my parents don't go into cardiac arrest when I tell them."

Rodney leaned against the wall, quietly picking his thumb. "Look," he said, finally. "Whatever's happened between you and Clue, don't let it ruin a good thing."

I glanced up, ready to throw on my best acting chops and pretend to not have any idea what he was talking about. But Rodney returned my stare with a knowing look.

"I see the way you two look at each other," he said. "Clue and I have been best mates for eight years, and I've never seen her go soft the way she does with you. She likes you; I can tell."

"So why do I get the feeling she hates my guts?"

Rodney shrugged, thinking. "She's been through a lot," he said. "I know that's not an excuse, but it does make sense. Ever since her dad left, she's been a bit of a loner. Afraid of getting close to people again, I think. And now with Miss P...." Rodney sighed. *If you don't get close, then you can't get hurt.* That's Clue's motto."

"That's a terrible motto."

"I know."

Clue came shuffling back a few minutes later. Way too soon for my liking, because I was nowhere near ready to make that phone call. When

Rodney and I headed for the cell door, however, Officer Daniels held up a hand. We stepped back as the bars rolled shut again.

"No need," he said, nodding toward Clue. "Your co-conspirator here spoke for you. You all should be out of here soon enough." He shook his head, annoyed, and walked away.

"What's going on?" I asked.

"What's happening, C?" said Rodney. "What did you do?"

Clue crossed her arms, leaned against the far wall, and looked up at the ceiling as a heavy sigh escaped her lips. There must've been a good reason why we weren't allowed our phone calls — not that I was in any rush to break the news to my parents. Still, if I was going to be denied my one chance at contact with the outside world, I wanted to at least know why.

Finally, Clue coughed it up.

"I spoke to Dad," she said. "I told him everything."

Rodney's mouth fell wide open. *"Everything?"*

"That's not all," said Clue, squeezing herself tighter. She was practically squirming.

Rodney and I waited for her to continue. We didn't move. We barely breathed.

"He's coming here. To get us."

CHAPTER 66

I never got another chance to give Clue my letter. Rodney didn't shut up long enough for me to even try. He kept asking Clue questions about her dad — *Is he angry? Do you think he remembers me? Did you really tell him we stole his star? Is he pressing charges? Is he going to tell our parents? Wonder what his net worth is now?* — and by the time he took a breather, I was too anxious myself about Mr. Perez's arrival that all I could focus on was slow breathing techniques and swallowing waves of nausea.

"Looking a little green over there, sonny."

Crazy Eyes' cackling voice wormed its way into my ears. When I turned, he was pressed against his bars again, licking his gums and smiling wickedly. Like he wanted to see me hurl.

He chuckled. "Deny everything. That's my advice."

"That's enough."

It was Officer Daniels, stepping through the door at the perfect moment. I never thought I'd be happy to see him, but his timing was much appreciated. He unlocked our cell door and motioned for us to follow him to the front lobby.

"There's someone here to see you."

Seeing Mr. Perez for the first time in person (I'd seen him plenty online) was the equivalent of meeting the King of England or shaking hands with Morgan Freeman. I'm guessing.

Mr. Perez had that special celebrity quality, that X Factor — and not just because of his designer coat and shoes. His presence was strong and powerful. Standing there in the middle of the police station lobby, it was as if he were the sun and everyone else simply revolved around him.

If this were one of those cheesy Christmas movies, he'd probably be *glowing*.

But there was no glow in Clue's eyes. They were dark and unknowing, as if she didn't recognize the man standing before us. As if she hadn't just called him half an hour ago.

"Cluenette?" Mr. Perez began, before catching himself. "I mean…Clue?"

I couldn't pull my eyes away from her. I stood nearby and watched as her nostrils flared, as her eyes misted at the sound of her dad's voice saying her name. Something she hadn't heard in a very long time.

"Dad…."

Her voice slipped out in a whisper. Surprisingly without any edge. Without hate. And without any hint of bitterness.

And then they were hugging, meeting each other in the middle of the lobby underneath the blinking fluorescent lights, surrounded by me, Rodney, and a circle of police officers anxious to meet the famous Emelio Perez. And that's when it hit me: This whole charade — all of the climbing and stealing and sneaking around — it wasn't just about New York remembering her. In some way, it was also about Clue's dad finally noticing her.

It was about getting his attention.

CHAPTER 67

"Sooo…will you be suing us, Mr. P? Or how does this work exactly?"

The four of us were seated in the back of a black stretch limousine — complements of Mr. Perez — and although Rodney was dead serious, I couldn't help smiling at his question. Clue sat next to her dad on the far leather bench; a small grin broke loose from her as well.

"Well, Rodney," said Mr. Perez, leaning forward and clasping his hands together. His gold Rolex and rings glimmered in the passing city lights. "Since Clue has agreed to tell me where you three hid my star, I was thinking we could skip the whole suing thing."

Rodney nodded but remained silent.

"Unless you'd like to be sued?"

"No, no!" said Rodney. "Your first suggestion was brilliant. No suing sounds…brilliant."

Mr. Perez leaned back in his seat, chuckling. "I thought you'd like that," he said. "And I won't be telling your parents either."

Rodney's eyes nearly doubled in size, and my ears definitely perked up at the news.

"You won't?" said Rodney.

"No. I'll leave that job to you."

Mr. Perez looked between Rodney and me. I nodded.

"That's fair…," Rodney admitted, aimlessly spinning the lens cover of his returned camera.

"Thank you, sir," I said.

"While I can't condone what you all did, I am thankful my daughter has such a close-knit group of friends who are willing to stand by her side. Of course," said Mr. Perez, "I would prefer you to stand on the *legal* side of society in the future." He sighed and gave Clue a gentle, almost sorrowful smile. "Besides," he continued, "I've made my own share of mistakes. I'm hoping we can all receive a little extra grace tonight."

The limo continued up Madison Avenue — cruising past some giant cathedral, past several designer stores whose names I vaguely recognized, and past at least a dozen window displays full of fancy jewelry. Pieces you'd expect to find on the necks of the Royal Family.

Definitely in Rodney's neighborhood, I thought.

Sure enough, the limo rounded the block onto Fifth Avenue, and moments later the driver was pulling to the curb. Rodney slid out onto the sidewalk, but before going, he threw up a peace sign and snapped a group selfie with his camera. A memento of our special night.

"Good to see you again, Mr. P."

Mr. Perez nodded. He seemed to be holding back another chuckle. "You as well, Rodney."

Rodney looked from Clue to me, unsure of how to proceed. And I didn't blame him. What happened now? What next? We'd been rolling this snowball uphill all week...and now it was suddenly careening down the other side.

"Well, it's been quite the ride, you two," he said after a brief silence. "Goodbye."

"Rodney," I said, just as he was shutting the door. He stopped. "Aunt Celeste's Broadway debut is tomorrow night. She got us three tickets. Think you can make it?"

Rodney pulled off his beanie and sighed. "I'd love to, mate, but let's face it. Mum's going to murder me when she finds out I've been in the cop shop. Or at least ground me for eternity." He shrugged and looked genuinely bummed. "Sorry."

My stop was up next. We crossed the Brooklyn Bridge, leaving the twinkling lights of the city behind as we snaked our way to Sunset Park. Half-burned-out neon signs and dirty bodegas were a far cry from the gold and limestone façades of Fifth Avenue. If Clue hadn't also lived in the neighborhood, I'd probably be more embarrassed in front of our world-famous carpool buddy.

"I could've taken the subway," I reminded him.

"Nonsense," said Mr. Perez. "You three have had quite the night already. Plus," he added, "Clue and her mother are nearby. I'd like to stop in if..." He gave Clue his full attention. Nodded. "If that's alright..."

There were very few times when Clue was lost for words — and this seemed to be one of them. Her eyes darted toward me, but just as quickly, she looked away again. From my seat, I could see her anxiously chewing the inside of her cheek.

And then it hit me.

He doesn't know.

He doesn't know about Mrs. Perez. He doesn't know she's sick.

How could he? It had been four years since he'd last seen her, and from what I'd been told, from what I'd witnessed, Mrs. Perez wasn't exactly the same person. Not in certain ways.

"It's late," Clue finally said, still staring out the window. "She'll be asleep."

"Of course, of course." Mr. Perez glanced my way, probably hoping I wasn't paying attention, and then cleared his throat. "Maybe some other time."

As soon as I got out and closed the car door, the clock started ticking. I knew I only had minutes — five at most — to beat the limo. I waved goodbye, and as soon as Mr. Perez and Clue disappeared around the corner, I took off as fast as my string-bean legs would carry me.

Leftover slush from yesterday's snow still dotted the ground, now frozen. I skidded and slid from courtyard to courtyard, jumping over fences and racing across side streets and parking lots. I paused under a lamp pole; my breath came out in frosty vapors as my brain worked double-time to remember the way. I'd only been to Clue's twice and never by such sketchy means.

This way!

I trusted my memory, and finally I saw it — the four-story brick apartment complex. I'd recognize that rusty chain-link fence anywhere. The limo was still nowhere in sight, so I dashed across the street and sprinted up the steps.

13.

I stopped in front of apartment thirteen and swallowed. Breathed. And suddenly, as I stood in a cold sweat staring at the peeling door, it was as if I was falling into a warm, fuzzy dream. I pictured the room beyond and all the memories held there: Clue and Rodney racing around a smoky kitchen, dumping handfuls of charred toast in the trash. Me comforting sweet Mrs. Perez. Clue decorating the tree. Her and I sitting side by side on the couch. Laughing... Talking...

A burst of headlights flashed from somewhere outside. I blinked away the memories, and without wasting another second, I yanked the folded letter from my pocket and slipped it under the door.

CHAPTER 68

The doorbell rang around 10 a.m., just as I was pouring my second coffee and Aunt Celeste was working on her third cup of hot tea loaded with lemon and honey. *Good for the throat,* she'd said, patting her neck. *These delicate pipes need to be in tiptop shape tonight!*

Aunt Celeste had woken up at the crack of dawn, giddier than usual and humming the entire score of *Wicked.* As a result, I'd been forced to get up too — no matter how many pillows I'd used to try and drown out the noise.

"Who on earth?" Aunt Celeste remained seated, stirring in yet another spoonful of honey; her tea was probably the consistency of glue by now. She craned her neck to see the front door. "I wonder who that could be?"

"I'll check."

I glanced through the peephole, expecting to find a postal worker delivering goat food or something, but was surprised to see a very familiar bush of blonde hair waiting on the other side.

"Rodney?" I said, opening the door. "What's up? I thought you were grounded."

"Incredibly grounded," said Rodney. "Mum thinks I'm at school right now, though. Otherwise we wouldn't be here."

"We?"

Rodney scooted over, and before either of us could say another word, Clue emerged from the right. She stood there in the doorway, just inches away, her vanilla perfume already filling up the space between us.

"We," she said.

CHAPTER 69

I was so surprised to see Clue and Rodney — and to actually hear Clue willingly speak again — that I hadn't even noticed the brown paper bags they were carrying.

"What's all this?" I said, finally finding my tongue again.

"A surprise!" Rodney gave Clue a look, and she nodded for him to go on. "We got to thinking, and about halfway through first period, we decided we should be here to celebrate your aunt. It is her big day, after all!"

Just then, the actress herself appeared behind me — with teacup, blue hair, pink silk robe, and all. Up until that moment, in the presence of Clue and Rodney, I hadn't realized just how much Aunt Celeste resembled a walking cotton candy.

"Visitors!" she exclaimed. "Oh, Nate, are these your ice-skating friends you've been telling me about?"

"This would be them," I said, stepping aside.

Her eyes immediately landed on Clue. "Ah!" she said, clutching a hand to her chest. "It's you! The girl" — Aunt Celeste started snapping her fingers, trying to jog her memory — "the girl with the trash!"

It was true. Aunt Celeste had seen the whole thing: Me chasing after the dump truck. Me climbing *out* of the dump truck. Me handing Clue the slimy garbage bag full of star parts.

Clue gave a little bow. "That's me," she said dryly. "Just...just a trashy girl."

Rodney and I couldn't help but snicker.

"Well, come in *come in*," said Aunt Celeste, waving everyone inside. "It's freezing out here."

Rodney was all too eager to follow — but not before Clue whacked him with her grocery bag. Punishment for laughing. "Take this inside, would you? I need to talk to Nate." She turned to me. "If that's alright."

"Of course."

I closed the door behind Aunt Celeste and Rodney, leaving us alone on the landing.

Clue stuffed her hands inside her coat pockets. She took a deep breath. "I'm sorry for just showing up like this. We wanted it to be a surprise. Hopefully it's not too stalkerish."

"Not at all," I laughed. "I'm glad y'all came. But" — I shrugged and felt myself cutting eyes around the place — "how did you find us?"

Clue bit her bottom lip. "Google," she finally admitted, with a little grin. "Rodney searched for like two seconds and found it." As soon as the words escaped her, Clue grimaced and put a hand to her forehead. "Oh, gosh, we're totally stalkers, aren't we?"

"No, it's fine. Seriously. I'm...I'm glad you came."

Clue suddenly became very quiet. She swallowed. "I got your letter," she almost whispered. And then added, "Nate, I'm so sorry for freaking out on you. I—"

"It's okay."

"No, it's not," she said. I could feel her fumbling, wading through whatever emotions were hiding near the surface. "I treated you so badly. And for what? All you did was write nice things about me. You helped us with the star. You were there for Mom when she needed someone." Clue scoffed at herself. "You got us a *tree* for crying out loud."

"Well, to be fair, I didn't have much say in the whole star ordeal."

Clue shook her head, unable to keep from smiling. "You're right," she said. "Sorry about that too."

A beat passed before either of us spoke.

"Are we good?" I had to know.

As if the day wasn't weird enough already, Clue — *the* Clue Perez — reached for *my* hand. "I hope so." Tears immediately filled her brown eyes. "I am sorry," she said again. "I don't hate your words...and I don't hate you." The tears, teetering on the edge, finally spilled down her cheeks. "I was just scared of getting too close," she whispered, looking down at her boots now. "People I care about. They always seem to…"

To disappear. One way or another.

Her dad.

Her mom.

Gently, I lifted Clue's chin until our eyes met again. Until we were locked in and focused. With no distractions. "It's okay," I repeated. "I'm not going anywhere. Not if you don't want me to."

A faint smile tickled her lips. Another tear rolled its way down.

And before another thought or word or breath passed between us, Clue and I were both leaning in. My eyes closed, and I was ready. I'd thought about this moment plenty of times —

"Come on, you two!"

Aunt Celeste. Yanking open the door.

"Today is glorious," she trilled. "I can't be rushing you to the ER for hypothermia!"

CHAPTER 70

Aunt Celeste was off from work today. The *Wicked* cast had apparently rehearsed their brains out for months — definitely this past week — and the director was giving them the whole day to rest their voices before tonight's show.

So, technically, Aunt Celeste *did* have time to hit up the ER.

Which meant she *didn't* have to interrupt my chance at almost kissing Clue.

Oh, well.

Aunt Celeste, Clue, and I piled onto the small couch while Rodney took the chair. We kept the living room lights off, opting for just the rosy glow of the pink Christmas tree. There was some debate over what to watch — *White Christmas* or *It's a Wonderful Life* — but since today was all about Aunt Celeste, we decided to go with option one. Her favorite.

"There's simply no beating *White Christmas*," she explained. "The music alone is topnotch. And Mr. Crosby... Mm, that man was a dream!"

Of course, Gerdy had to get in on the action too. She stared up at Clue with giant, watery goat eyes until Clue inched over all she could. Gerdy didn't hesitate. As soon as she saw empty real estate, she sprang onto the couch, nestling her fresh-diaper-bottom between Clue and me.

"Hey, Pampers," said Clue, scratching the soft spot between Gerdy's ears. "How's it going, girl?"

Thirty minutes into the movie, the oven timer started beeping.

Clue slid off the couch. "Got it! Be back in a sec."

She returned a few minutes later in a wave of cinnamon. The entire apartment smelled like it — warm and spicy, sweet and delicious. She set down the pan she was carrying and removed her oven mitts.

"Congratulations again," she said, beaming.

Aunt Celeste clasped her hands together in surprise, as if she'd just won a Tony. "Oh, my stars!" she squealed. "That is too thoughtful. You all shouldn't have!"

"Congratulations, Aunt C!" said Rodney.

I wrapped an arm around her. "Congrats, Aunt Celeste."

On the coffee table was a round pan of fresh cinnamon rolls, piping hot. And in white letters of ooey gooey icing were the words GOOD LUCK, AUNT C!

We ate until we were sick and left no crumbs behind.

CHAPTER 71

Aunt Celeste offered to take me to the theater earlier that evening with her. She'd be busy, of course, prepping and getting makeup and hair done, but she said I was more than welcome to tag along. "Maybe explore backstage a bit before the show?"

It was tempting; it really was. But getting the chance to personally escort Clue to Broadway? That was a no-brainer.

Before Clue and Rodney left Aunt Celeste's that afternoon, we'd made a plan.

Clue needed to fix dinner for her mom and get her settled before Miss Mable came back over for a few more hours. She'd already spent the entire school day with Mrs. Perez, like she usually did, but Clue reassured me she could still go to the show.

"Miss Mable won't mind," she said. "All she does is sit there on the couch with her knitting needles and basket of yarn. Which she'd be doing at her own place anyway. Actually," Clue confided, "she's told me more than once that she looks forward to staying over. Gives her some company too."

So it was settled. I'd pick Clue up at *six o'clock sharp*, and we'd head to the theater together, giving ourselves a few extra minutes before showtime to grab something from the snack bar. That was the plan — and boy did it feel good to plan something, for once, that didn't involve climbing a sixty-nine-foot tree and breaking the law.

Thankfully, I'd packed some halfway decent clothes for the show. A nice gray sweater, dark pants, and the black suede shoes Mom had found on sale at Kohl's last spring. I'd never worn them, but now seemed as good a time as any.

I was surprised when Mrs. Perez answered the door. A big smile spread across her face as soon as she swung it open.

"Hi, Mrs. Perez," I said, nodding. "It's good to see you again."

Mrs. Perez giggled, almost childishly. "Good to see you again too...um..."

"Nate, Mom," came Clue's voice. "Remember?"

Mrs. Perez put a finger to her mouth and nodded vigorously. "Oh, *yes*, of course. Hi, Nate. Hi there."

And that's when I saw her.

Clue.

Mrs. Perez, already in her nightgown, stepped away from the door, and that's when I saw her, a Clue I'd never laid eyes on before. One with makeup and pinned-up hair.

And a dress.

"Wow," I said. Because that's all I could say. My tongue suddenly felt ten sizes too big — and *numb* — like it'd been jabbed with a big dose of Novocaine. "You look...you look great," I finally sputtered. "Wow."

I was way out of my league. At least it felt that way. Like she was the princess and I was the ugly, wart-infested frog. I half expected my glasses to fog up from embarrassment. At least I'd gone with my gut at the last minute and thrown on a white oxford button-up under my sweater. That made it a *little* nicer. Right?

"Thanks," said Clue, running her hands down the gauzy fabric of her burgundy dress. She seemed nervous, which I completely understood, because I was battling a hundred swirling butterflies in the pit of my own stomach.

I swallowed, unsure how to proceed.

This was *Clue* for crying out loud. The girl who'd jumped me at the ice rink and twisted my arm until I agreed to help with her crazy scheme. The girl I'd risked my life climbing a tree for. Who I'd stolen for. Finally, I was free from all of that. Shouldn't I count my lucky stars and just be glad her dad sprung us from jail? Shouldn't I be running as far away as possible?

And yet...I couldn't.

As I watched her slide on a coat and say goodbye to her mom, I couldn't imagine walking away from this girl. This new friend.

And it wasn't just the dress.

CHAPTER 72

The lobby inside the Gershwin Theatre was a flurry of activity. Music played throughout as people scurried around in their fanciest clothes, taking pictures and oohing and ahhing over *Wicked* memorabilia behind glass cases.

Clue leaned in and muttered, "Glad we dressed up."

"You and me both."

It wasn't until we started climbing the first set of stairs that I noticed Clue was wearing her black combat boots. She lifted her dress to avoid tripping, and there they were in all their glory. I smiled without saying a word.

The seats Aunt Celeste had snagged for us were perfect. On the main floor, a little to the left, with an excellent stage view. But the best part was that since neither of my parents came, we had one empty seat beside us.

"Too bad Rodney couldn't make it," I said, nodding to the third seat. "I wonder what he's up to?"

"Well," said Clue, "Mrs. Donoghue probably took away his phone and camera, so I'd guess he's sleeping." She paused to sip her drink. "Or staring at his pictures maybe."

The sunset strings.

Rodney's collection of sunsets he'd captured from around the world.

I texted Aunt Celeste to wish her good luck, and before the lights dimmed, I convinced Clue to let me take a picture of her holding her *Wicked* Playbill. She immediately rolled her eyes, but the smile on my phone told me she was enjoying every moment.

And then it was showtime. A Munchkin with curly hair and an emerald-green suit skipped onto the stage to welcome everyone. As he dashed away, the wall sconces around the theater burned out...the audience hushed...and the orchestra burst into song.

"There she is!"

Clue was the first to spot Aunt Celeste. She pointed to the edge of the stage, where a thin woman in strips of brown and red clothing was prancing around. A citizen of Oz. At first I was disappointed I hadn't noticed my own flesh and blood, but the missing blue hair — now hidden beneath a floppy brown hat — and the cakey makeup threw me off.

The entire show was brilliant, but every time Aunt Celeste appeared, I hovered on the edge of my seat. I couldn't take my eyes off her. My spastic and (let's be honest) over-the-top aunt had disappeared, replaced by an incredible performer. Her arms and legs landed every move, keeping in perfect time with the music, and more than once I could've sworn I heard her soprano over every other voice.

"She's amazing," I heard Clue say during a big musical number.

I nodded, unable to tear my eyes away. She really was.

It didn't matter that Aunt Celeste wasn't gliding around stage in a tiara as Glinda the Good. Or Elphaba, soaring high on her broomstick in a puff of green smoke. She was singing and dancing her heart out. This was her dream. She'd left home with a mission, and she'd stuck to her guns. It was nice seeing her so happy, in her element.

The citizens of Oz finished another song, and as the final note rang out across the theater, their arms raised to the sky, I couldn't help but smile. Because isn't that exactly what I wanted? When you boiled it all down, I just wanted to write. I wanted to spend my days doing what I love.

I almost laughed right there in my seat. Aunt Celeste and I, it seemed, had a lot more in common than I'd ever realized.

CHAPTER 73

Before catching the subway back to Brooklyn, Clue insisted on showing me something. "Come on," she said. "Rockefeller Center's only two blocks away."

To be honest, I'd seen *plenty* of that place over the past few days to last me a lifetime. But I was up for anything with Clue.

"Sure," I said. "Let's do it."

Freezing wind whistled down 50th Street, squeezing between buildings and blasting us in the face. I burrowed my neck inside my coat collar.

"Almost there," said Clue, as we hurried under the red and gold marquee of Radio City Music Hall.

I was ready to go underground, to the warmth of the subway station. The choking stench of weed down there seemed like a better choice than freezing our ears off topside. But then we reached Rockefeller Plaza. We turned right — and every icycled bone in my body thawed.

There was the Rockefeller Center Christmas Tree wrapped in thousands of multicolored lights.

And there — right on top, by some miracle — was the star.

"Are you kidding me?" It had to be some kind of illusion. Some trick. "How…?"

Clue snuggled up next to me as we both continued staring. "Dad had his team work through the night to get it back up and running."

Back up and running?

She made it sound like a broken-down Camry that just needed its battery jumped.

But this? It didn't seem possible. Clue had sliced those spikes clean off. Last time I checked, the star looked like the underbelly of a silver colander, holes and all. But there it was now in all its glittering glory. All twelve spikes sparkling perfectly. Illuminating the entire plaza and every eager face gazing up at its beauty.

Like some kind of Christmas magic.

CHAPTER 74

It was almost midnight by the time we returned to Clue's apartment. Mrs. Perez was fast asleep in her room, and Miss Mable was conked out in the armchair, her gray head all lopsided on her shoulder but her fists still clutching her needles. Like she could resume knitting at any moment. Clue gently woke her, helped gather her belongings, and saw her to the door.

After hanging up our coats on a wooden rack, Clue asked, "Want some eggnog?"

"Yeah, that'd be great. But are you sure? It's pretty late."

"Of course." She returned from the kitchen a minute later carrying two cold glasses of frothy eggnog. She handed me one. "Mom and I used to make this together every Christmas when I was little. I'm trying to keep the tradition going."

I took a long, delicious swig while Clue walked over to her dad's record player and dropped the needle onto an old vinyl. Nat King Cole's "The

Christmas Song" crackled to life, and the apartment instantly felt cozier, like a warm hug you needed after a long day.

"This is the best eggnog I've ever had," I said, ready to down the last half. I only stopped when I saw Clue put a hand over her mouth, doing a terrible job at hiding a smile. "What is it?"

"You uh…" She tapped her top lip. "You've got a little something…"

I wiped the froth away with the sleeve of my sweater. "Thanks."

As she sipped her eggnog, Clue gazed at the record spinning round and round. There was something peaceful about her. A contentment that hadn't been there when we first met.

"What did you think of the show?" I asked.

She sighed thoughtfully. "Unreal. Seriously, it wasn't like anything I've ever seen before. The music. The whole production. *Your Aunt*." She shook her head. "I wish I could see it for the first time again."

"I know what you mean." I finished my eggnog, took care of any more foam mustaches, and set my glass on the coffee table. Then I held out a hand. "Would you like to dance?"

For once, I didn't give myself a chance to wonder whether she'd laugh or not. I just went with my gut, and in that moment, what I really wanted more than anything was to dance with Clue Perez.

She didn't laugh. She didn't smirk or scrunch up her nose or shake her head no. She didn't say anything at all. Instead, she set her glass down and slid her hand in mine.

And we danced.

Right there in her living room. In the warm, kaleidoscope glow of the Christmas tree. One hand holding hers, the other on her waist. With the great Nat King Cole to guide us.

We danced as if we had a million times before. We danced as if we'd known each other our whole lives.

Everything I'd been through with this girl in front of me felt like a lifetime already — and I realized I wouldn't trade it for the world. I wanted to hold on to it.

Wanted to hold on to *her*.

"Clue?"

My voice came out low and croaky from not speaking. We stopped swaying, and when she looked up at me — when I stared into those great brown eyes and memorized that sprinkling of freckles — I couldn't help myself any longer.

I leaned down. And I kissed her.

And she kissed me back.

CHAPTER 75

We fell into each other.

My hand found the back of her neck, and as I pulled her in close, we kept kissing. Her lips were as soft as I'd imagined. Like butter or velvet or rose petals or whatever else you could compare them to. All I knew is that they were perfect.

At some point we stopped, like an unspoken agreement between the two of us. We pulled away but held one another's gaze for a moment longer, both of us grinning a little giddily.

Heart pounding, I tucked a loose lock of hair behind her ear. "Was that okay?" I asked.

Clue said nothing. She nodded but didn't say a word.

And then tears filled her eyes, reflecting in the soft glow of the Christmas tree.

"What is it?" I put a hand up to her face again, and this time, she twisted her cheek into my palm, resting it there.

"You're leaving tomorrow."

Her quiet voice mimicked the pain now etched in her face. She kept her eyes squeezed shut, almost as if that would cancel my departure. Keep another person in her life from disappearing. The whole *If I can't see it, then it isn't real* mentality.

But it was real.

It wasn't one of my stories scribbled in my notebook. Trust me, if I could, I'd rewrite a whole new ending.

"I know…," I said. "And I'm sorry. I wish I didn't have to go."

I wrapped my arms around her and brought her in tight. It was crazy — someone so small could pack such a punch. Could take on the Rockefeller Center Christmas Tree like it was breakfast. Could wield a blowtorch better than any greasy mechanic.

From where I stood, there was nothing Clue *couldn't* do.

"It's okay," she said, resting her head on my chest. "It's just…weird how things change."

The understatement of the century.

"Yeah. Just last week I thought you were going to kill me. *And* the goat."

If she smiled, I never knew. Clue didn't say much else after that. We stayed just like we were — her ear to my heartbeat, us holding on to each other — the familiar scent of vanilla enveloping us as we swayed for a little while longer until it was really, really late.

And time for me to go home.

CHAPTER 76

Rodney's parents agreed to lift his grounding — just for an hour — so he could see me off at Penn Station with the rest of the crew. Afterward, the chauffer had strict orders to immediately drive him and Clue back to school.

"Mum said she'll be calling Principal Greybill this afternoon," Rodney said as we waited for my train to arrive. Then, in an annoyingly high-pitched voice meant to imitate Mrs. Donoghue, he added, *"To make sure you return promptly and resume your classes, which, of course, are most important."*

I shook my head. That was her all right.

"Thanks again for coming, Rodney. It means a lot."

"Of course!" he said, releasing me from a hug. "Couldn't let our best cellmate go without saying goodbye, could we?" And in the blink of an eye, like he was sometimes prone to do, he turned on Serious Rodney Mode and clapped a hand on my shoulder. "Only a true friend would've done what you did for us this week," he said solemnly. "If we meet again someday...I owe you. *Big* time."

Suddenly, an announcement echoed throughout the station.

"TRAIN 176 TO VIRGINIA WITH INTERMITTENT STOPS NOW BOARDING THROUGH GATE 15. TRAIN 176 NOW BOARDING."

"Nate," said Aunt Celeste, hurrying over with Gerdy by her side, "you're sure you have everything? Phone charger? Snacks? Water bottles?"

I laughed. "Be careful, Aunt Celeste. You're starting to sound like Mom."

"Ha! Even so, I'm still the coolest aunt around. You just remember that."

"Always," I said.

For someone who only cries when necessary for the occasional audition — and whose sole response to my arrest was a story about the time *she* was incarcerated in *Vegas* for 72 hours over an

"Elvis incident" at the Little White Chapel — tears immediately filled Aunt Celeste's eyes.

"Ohhh, *come here*," she choked, reaching and squeezing me fiercely. "It's been a delight having you stay with me."

"Thanks, Aunt Celeste. Good luck with the rest of your shows. I love you."

"I love you too," she said, patting my cheek before picking up Gerdy. "And Gerdy Girl says she'll miss you sooooo much!"

Aunt Celeste waved one of Gerdy's front hooves, so I politely gave it a little shake.

"ONCE AGAIN, THIS IS A BOARDING CALL FOR TRAIN 176 TO VIRGINIA. PLEASE PROCEED TO GATE 15."

"Well," I said, sliding on my bag. "I'd better go."

It's like they somehow knew. Rodney and Aunt Celeste. It's like they knew Clue and I needed one last moment together. One last goodbye. Without any goofy looks or side comments, they both slowly drifted away, and Clue walked with me as I rolled my luggage to the escalator leading down to Gate 15. We stood there at the top, the moveable stairs e x p a n d i n g and contracting, e x p a n d i n g and contracting as they made their descent.

We both stood in silence and watched the stairs. Listened to their rhythmic hum and click. The final thing that would pull us away from each other.

There wasn't a lot of time, and with that kind of pressure, the first coherent thing that popped into my mind wasn't great.

"I guess this is it then."

"I guess so," said Clue, crossing the arms of her puffy black coat and grinning weakly.

She was back in her overalls, just like that first night we met out on the ice. But everything else had changed.

We had changed.

"I wish we had more time —" I started, but Clue shook her head. Closed her eyes.

"It's okay. You don't need to say anything. Just —" She released the biggest sigh, and when she finished, she practically lunged on top of me, wrapping her arms around me in the biggest bearhug.

"Just take care of yourself," she whispered in my chest.

"FINAL BOARDING CALL FOR TRAIN 176. PASSENGERS FOR TRAIN 176, THIS IS YOUR FINAL BOARDING CALL."

We'd run out of time. This was the end for us.

The very thought wrenched its way into my chest, like a knife twisting through every layer of my heart.

As we held on tightly one last time, I kissed the top of Clue's head. I could smell her shampoo. Her skin. Her vanilla.

"I won't forget you, Clue Perez," I whispered. *"I promise."*

No matter who else did. Her dad. Her mom. Every borough in New York City.

I wouldn't forget.

The tears came quickly, hot and stinging, but I didn't let her see. I stepped onto the escalator with my luggage and didn't look back, no matter how badly I wanted to, as it carried me away.

And that's when I let myself cry.

CHAPTER 77

Eight hours of pure torture.

That pretty much summed up the train ride home.

And it wasn't just because the heating system decided to keel over and die that day, turning the train car into a flying icebox pushing ninety down the tracks. Or the fact that the train itself was at full capacity, meaning I was the lucky guest that Chubs chose to squeeze in and sit beside.

Thankfully, I'd snagged a window seat — not that it mattered much.

Trees and homes and little towns whisked by, but the only flashes of color I noticed were those of the past week. The green of Rockefeller Center Christmas Tree. Flailing around in a blue ninja costume. Speeding *Fast & Furious*-style in a yellow taxi. Aunt Celeste's orange coat. Rodney's sunsets. Clue's jet-black hair. Her brown eyes. Her cinnamon skin…

Another sigh escaped me.

Leaning back in my seat, I closed my eyes and let the tape roll. What had started as the scariest week of my life turned out to be the greatest. And then it was gone.

They were gone.

She was gone.

All I had now were the memories.

CHAPTER 78

Everyone told me the pain, the sadness, the whatever-it-was I felt when I returned to Virginia would get better over time — and I guess it did.

Chores replaced plotting and scheming. School carpool replaced my short career as a taxi-stealing road hog. And helping wash dishes for Mom's catering business practically every weekend left me little time to climb giant Christmas trees.

I thought about Clue and Rodney every single day at first...but then weeks turned to months. And months trickled into years.

Life charged ahead, changing with the seasons, and eventually the day came where I wasn't obsessing over that week in New York. I didn't have *time* to.

High school graduation came and went. The University of Virginia accepted me into their creative writing program, and my parents were actually super supportive, if not a little apprehensive. Every few months Mom would drag out the We-Could-Be-Catering-Partners speech, but sometime around the start of junior year, the suggestion stopped. She knew where my heart lie. They both did.

That being said, I never forgot about Clue and Rodney. I couldn't if I tried.

They were always there, waiting in the wings of my mind, ready to remind me of our adventures at any given moment.

And I welcomed those memories like an old friend.

Six Years Later...

EPILOGUE

Six Years Later

It's strange being back in New York for business. Last time I was here, I landed in jail and nearly plunged to my death falling out of the Rockefeller Center Christmas Tree.

I smile at the thought.

Don't get me wrong — that whole disaster was anything *but* funny. One of those we'll-look-back-at-this-one-day-and-laugh moments.

I guess that day has come.

New York City in December is just as frigid as I remember, even with a long *Doctor Who* wool coat. At least this time I had sense enough to wear thick boots and socks. The wind is howling down the street today, so I don't tarry. I burrow down in my turtleneck and plow forward. I round a vaguely familiar corner…and there it is.

Java the Hut.

Same green door. Same goofy sign with the same silhouette of a certain slug alien holding a steaming cup of joe.

I click off my earbuds, slide my phone into my pocket, and duck inside.

Smooth jazz plays throughout the café, muffling some of the honking horns outside. After ordering, I find a table near the picture window and shed my bag and coat. A barista delivers my coffee soon after. I take a few sips as I watch the commotion out on the street, and it's delicious. Piping hot and just sweet enough.

Wind chimes jingle, signaling a new customer. I glance across the café as the newcomer makes her way toward the front counter — and I almost spit out my coffee.

Is that —?

No.

I swallow and set my coffee down before I make a mess.

There's no way....

The girl tosses her dark hair back as she orders, and she says something to the workers behind the counter that garners everyone's attention and laughter. I sit there, staring, waiting for her to turn around. Waiting to see...

"Clue?"

Her eyes meet mine. She blinks several times, like she needs to clear her contacts to make sure she's seeing correctly. The sunlight hits her brown eyes, turning them almost amber-gold, and I know it's her.

She smiles. "*Nate?* Is that you?"

"Yeah," I say, just about swallowing my Adam's Apple, "it's me."

"I don't believe it," she gushes.

And then we hug like no time has passed at all. We hold each other, and that same vanilla scent wraps itself around me, transporting me back to all those years ago. Back to her living room. Back to our last goodbye.

"Whoa," she says when we finally pull away. "Somebody grew into themselves." She gives my bicep a tiny punch.

"Finally," I chuckle.

I invite her to sit with me, if she has time, and we catch up on everything. She tells me Rodney moved back to Australia like he always wanted and takes the most beautiful pictures.

"Look," she says, pulling out a cellphone and scrolling through photos. "He's had them published in magazines and everything."

"Hang on — is that *your* phone?" I lean back and whistle. "Miracles do happen, I guess."

"Shut up," she says, smiling.

And that's when she tells me about her dad. How he changed. How he got more involved. How he even insisted on paying for architecture school.

"And your mom?" I ask. "How is she?"

Clue picks at an empty sugar packet, tearing it up and rolling it between her fingers until it's just a tiny ball. "She passed away about two years ago."

"Clue..." I reach across the table and lay a hand on hers. "I'm so sorry. I had no idea."

"It's okay," she says, looking up with misty eyes. "You know she never forgot who I was? Even during that last week. She really struggled to remember much of anything, but she always called me her 'special little girl.' At least she knew that much."

"That's great." I could feel my own eyes starting to burn, thinking about sweet Mrs. Perez. *Gone.* "I'm glad you have that to hold on to."

Clue wipes the tears from her cheeks. "So," she says, clearing her throat, "what about you? What are you doing here in the city?"

"Actually" — I dig through my messenger bag and retrieve the book — "I'm here on tour."

"Excuse me?"

I slide the hardback toward her. "This is mine. I've got a reading and signing tonight at the New York Public Library."

"This is yours?" she says, feeling the book's cover and turning it over and over in her hands, like it's some kind of magical object. "You wrote a book. Are you *kidding* me? That's incredible!" She rubs her thumb over my name, quietly taking it in. "I knew you would do it."

"Thanks. I'm glad someone did because I definitely had my doubts."

"*Robbin' Around the Christmas Tree...,*" she says, reading the title. "So?" Her bright eyes search my face. It's cute seeing her practically burst at the seams. *"What's it about?"*

After finishing my coffee, I set the cup back on the saucer and slide the whole thing to the edge of our table. "Us."

"Us?"

"Us," I repeat, unable to stifle a grin. "Me. You. Rodney. The names are changed and everything, of course, but it's our story. Our adventures here in the city."

Clue looks anything but angry. Actually, she looks speechless, so I nod toward the book in her hands.

"Open it."

She does. She opens it slowly, page by page. First the cover, then the title page, then the copyright…and then the dedication.

Her bottom lip trembles as she reads, and when she looks up at me, her eyes are swimming in tears. She reads the dedication again, quietly to herself.

For Clue.
I told you I'd never forget.

I remember typing those words years ago, even before I'd sold the book. Her name. Permanently stamped in ink. A small gesture for the girl who was so afraid of being forgotten.

"You should come tonight," I offer. "To the reading. I'm no Augustine Grant, but it might be fun."

Clue says nothing for the longest time. She keeps rereading the dedication, weeping silently, and wiping away tears. Lost in the words. When she's finally ready, she closes the book, looks me directly in the eyes, and whispers words I didn't think existed in her vocabulary. Words I never dreamed she'd say.

"I think I love you, Nate Wilder."

I think I love you.

I remember how fast my heart beat the first time we climbed Rockefeller Center Christmas Tree. I remember the rush of adrenaline, the thrill and uncertainty of it all.

That was nothing compared to the pounding in my chest right now.

My hands find Clue's; they're soft and small and still so perfect. And I realize I want to kiss every single one of her freckles, even after all these years.

I want to keep making memories with her.

"I love you too."

ACKNOWLEDGMENTS

The book you now hold in your hands is the culmination of three years' work — but my writing journey, as a whole, goes back much further. I'm talking *decades*. And those who have stuck by my side throughout the years (some human, some not) deserve to be thanked.

First and foremost — always — thank you, God.

Thank you, Mom and Dad, for being my loudest cheerleaders. Were it not for your constant love, support, and prayers, this book would probably still be hidden on my computer, unfinished.

Thank you to my friends and family who held me accountable by asking for updates and praying over me.

Thank you, Mickey D's, for supplying me with much-needed caffeine in the form of many, many mocha frappes.

And thank you, Little Bisc. You were the best writing buddy a guy could ever have.

Sam Campbell began writing his first novel at the age of fourteen, which was (surprise surprise) total garbage. He hopes he has improved since then. When he's not writing, he likes to read, work out, and watch movies with his family. He also suffers from a terrible addiction to McDonald's frappes. Mocha, of course.

Made in the USA
Middletown, DE
10 December 2024

66633981R00234